Penny in London

FISHER AMELIE

For legal purposes, we are required to include this note from Graham Glenn:

Piss off, Penelope Beckett!

Penny in London

FISHER AMELIE

One over, please.

The hour, the minute, the second.

To my readers, with incredible gratitude and love.

Chapter One

Denial
[dih-**nahy**-uh l]
noun
1. An assertion that something said, believed, alleged, etc., is false.

Penelope Beckett is in denial. No, not the river in Africa.

Graham's hand sat on my waist. His long, slender fingers wrapped around the bone of my hip. He tucked me into his side and I almost melted into him. I imagined myself a stick of malleable butter, vulnerable to warm fingers slipping over the surface of my skin. Wherever he pressed, I would fold readily, happily. Wherever he touched, I would mold myself, eager and pliable and at his command.

"Who are we meeting up with?" I asked him, gazing

up as we walked toward the Chelsea Potter, a pub around the corner from our shared London flat.

"Just a few of the lads," he offered.

I sighed. "So Oliver will be there then," I said.

He pulled me into his arms and laughed. "Yes, love, Oliver'll be there." He let go of me. "What exactly do you hate about him so much then?"

"I don't *hate* him. Not at all, actually. I'm just not a fan, Graham. He's a womanizer," I argued for the millionth time since I'd met Oliver Finn.

Graham laughed, wrapped his arm around me again, and kissed my temple. "The women never seem to mind," he jabbed with his posh London accent.

"Graham," I protested, pulling away from him. He wouldn't have it, though, and pulled me back into his embrace. "There's something about him I don't trust," I explained.

"He's a nice enough bloke. Let him be, Penelope."

"He's charming, yes, but there's something there he's not letting us in on, and it's damaged. Nobody's that reckless without a reason."

"Why do Americans always break down a person?" he teased. "Not everyone has a secret past. Not everyone is that complicated."

"I know that. I'm just saying Oliver seems to be covering up something he doesn't want anyone to know about, and he does it by sleeping with every woman who will throw a look his way."

Graham laughed. "Let it be, Penelope."

I sighed and relented. "Fine, okay."

We approached the pub's green creaky door.

"Give us a kiss then, love." He bent me back and kissed

my lips then ushered me inside.

He tucked a loose hair from my French twist behind my ear. I rolled my eyes at this tiresome habit. He liked me well kept, always put together, never a hair out of place. Graham let me go when he approached his friends and stuck his arms out at his sides.

"Lock up your sisters, lads, I'm here!"

Whatever.

"Graham!" they all sang at once, slinking their chairs in closer to one another and pilfering a lonely chair at a nearby table for Graham.

"Sorry, Penny," Oliver teased, "you'll just have to settle in my lap. How's that then?" he asked, sitting back, his arms extended.

"Shut it, Oli," I said, perching myself on Graham's lap.

Graham stood up quickly, almost pitching me onto the floor. If Oliver hadn't caught my arm, I would have done just that.

"*Careful*, mate," Oli bit out at Graham, his brows furrowed.

Graham looked down at me, had the decency to look sheepish, and grabbed me by the upper arm to help me up. "Sorry, love. Be right back," he said, distracted. "Forgot a few of my work chums were coming 'round. I see a few of them now. Let me catch up." He looked down at me. "You'll be all right here?" he asked.

"Yeah," I answered, taking his chair.

Oli pushed my chair in for me while Graham sprinted for the door.

"Easily distracted," I explained to Oli, my cheeks a little pink with embarrassment.

"Like my granny's miniature poodle, that one," he

offered, making me laugh.

Oliver peered over at the bar.

"Who's on the docket tonight?" I asked him, perusing the girls myself, trying to decide which one he'd go for. I spotted a blonde with big boobs in the corner. "Let me guess," I told him, gesturing toward my pick. "Her?"

He strained his neck trying to see who I'd chosen in the busy pub.

"Who? Kate Moss wannabe?" he asked, laughing.

"Well, yeah," I answered. "Most boys would think she's kind of a catch."

"Nah, not my type."

"Oh, as if you have a type?" I scoffed.

"I've a type, Penny," he stated with strength.

I swallowed at his tone. "I've never seen you discriminate, Oli."

He smiled that charismatic, devilish smile that got him all the girls and the intensity between us dissipated. "I'm an equal opportunity lover," he threw out like a baseball pitch.

I readied my bat. "That you are. On a completely unrelated note, have you been tested?"

He pretended to be wounded by my jab. "Clean as a whistle."

I shook my head at him. "You're lucky then."

"Okay, *Mum*."

"Do I look like your mom?" I asked him, a hand at my chest.

He looked at my hair. "That hair *is* tidy, Penny. My granny still wears it that way. Classic."

Feigning outrage, my hand went to my head. "Graham likes it this way."

Oliver pretended to straighten a jacket on his shoulders and pushed up an imaginary tie. "I'm Graham," he mocked. "Pleased to meet you, madam." Oliver studied my face and gasped. "Is that liner on your eye! For shame!"

I couldn't help but laugh. "I agree he is a bit fussy."

"Only a bit?" he snipped.

I smoothed my clothes as if Graham could be nearby, though he wasn't, not that I could see anyway. "He is *particular.*"

"And you particularly dish yourself up like a little Graham doll."

"What's wrong with wanting to please my boyfriend?" I asked him.

"Nothing, if pleasing him doesn't waste away at who you are," he answered curtly.

I felt my cheeks burn. His comment hit a little too close for comfort. "You think I'm betraying myself?" I asked in an unusual attempt at civility with Oliver.

All the color drained from his face. He cleared his throat. "I'm sorry, Penelope. That was out of line."

I nodded, not wanting to talk about it anymore. Instead, I turned toward the bar.

"That one," I offered to him.

A new girl. A little on the short side. She had brown hair, pretty teeth, and a sweet smile.

"I'd try her on, yeah."

"I knew you had a type," I said, elbowing him.

"I said I'd try her on. I never said she was my type."

Surprised, I asked, "What *does* your type look like, Oliver?"

He laughed, genuinely laughed. Like a gut laugh, and

it shocked me a little. I'd never really seen Oliver do anything that didn't show me how overly aware he was of himself.

"You don't want to know my type, Penny," he told me.

He stood up and headed toward the bar, but not before placing a hand on my head and ruining my twist.

"Oliver Finn!" I yelled at him.

"You'll get over it easily enough," he said.

I caught his arm and yanked him back toward me. I started to take all the bobby pins from my hair and gathered them into a pile on the table next to an old pint glass. "That was rude," I told him.

"Yeah? What's it matter to me then? You'll be gone in a few months' time. Just like the rest."

I flinched as if he'd hit me and let my hands fall to my lap. He stood stock-still, his face blank.

I leaned over the table toward Graham's friend Alfie and told him, "Tell Graham I'll meet him at home later, will ya?"

"Sure, love," he told me, engrossing himself in his previous conversation.

I stood up, left my pins at the table, and made my way toward the door. I felt someone's hands, Oliver's, grapple at my clothing, but I ignored them. I was going home.

Anger

[**Ang**-ger]

   noun

   1. A strong feeling of displeasure and belligerence aroused by a wrong; wrath; ire.

Graham Glenn is a proper prat whose philandering ways have courted the anger of one Miss Penelope Beckett.

Three months later...

"I love you so much, Graham. You're my everything," I told him.

"You're drunk, darling. Hush," Graham secreted into my ear.

Graham held me up, so he could have had a point. I attempted to boop his nose with my finger but missed. Yup, he was right. I looked up into his face. "Don't you love me back?" I asked.

He looked at me with pity and the humiliation this caused sobered me slightly. I stood tall. Well, as tall as my five-foot-seven-inch frame could stand next to his six-foot-four one. "Oh," I realized. "*You don't*, do you?"

"I'm sorry, Penelope, but I've met someone else," he said, wounding me into a clean, clear mind.

"Oh, that's too bad," I said, stumbling back. I rested my tired soul against a nearby lamppost, sinking down until my rear end met the larger base.

"I'm sorry, darling."

My glassy eyes met his steady ones. "I moved all the way here for you."

Standing collected and looking perfectly English, Graham tucked his scarf into his buttoned jacket. I studied my black tights. There was a hole at the knee. *How did that get there?* I wondered. My burgundy pleated skirt was wrinkled at the hem from where I'd gripped it earlier. I always did this when I was around Graham. It was unconscious, as if I was constantly bracing myself for news. It was an insecurity, or so I thought. Apparently that feeling was warranted. I looked at him again.

"I realize how inconvenient that is, darling," he assuaged.

I fought the urge to vomit at his feet. "Please stop calling me that."

He sighed as if I was a petulant child. "Penelope," he called out. He always used my full name. That was Graham, always so formal. "I'll need you out of my flat by Monday evening, preferably before I return home from work."

Tears fell. "Where should I go?" I asked, incredulous.

"I'll leave a few hundred pounds on our wardrobe," he

said. *Our wardrobe. Our wardrobe* kept running through my mind on a loop. "It should be enough to get you back to Dallas."

I looked at him, wondering who he was, wondering what had happened to the man who'd begged me to join him in London, wondering where the one who promised me forever had gone.

He started to walk away, but I called out to him. "Where are you going?" I asked.

"To her house," he answered. A bullet of the tongue that ran sharply through my struggling heart.

"Who is she?" I asked him, just to keep him near me. It all felt so abrupt.

"A girl from work."

Graham's work friends ran through my head, spinning until it landed on one face in particular.

"It's Chloe, isn't it?" I asked him.

He rolled his shoulders. He always did this when he was uncomfortable. I had my answer before he even spoke.

"Does it matter?" he asked. I didn't answer and he sighed. "Yes, it's Chloe."

I nodded my head. Chloe. Ample-chested, round-hipped, heart-shape-faced Chloe. Blonde Chloe. French Chloe. My-total-opposite Chloe.

"I can see the appeal," I told him, standing up. I smoothed my skirt, examined my Mary Jane heels, tucked in my cream silk blouse, and caught the loose pieces of my hair, tucking them back into my French twist. I jerked my fingers back. I only wore my hair that way because Graham insisted I wear it that way. My hands found my hair once again and pulled the pins out, letting them fall to my feet, raining little black pieces of metal. I shook my long black curled hair and let it spill over my shoulders.

Graham rolled his eyes at me. "Does that bother you, Graham?" I asked. "No longer yours to fuss over, though. Not anymore."

I shooed him away with my deep red lacquered nails, a color he picked out. He stood there, instead, and watched me. In an act of defiance, I untucked my blouse, unbuttoning it at the top, and exposed my nude-colored camisole. My hands reached up my skirt and yanked down my thigh-high black hose, letting it droop at my ankles over the straps of my heels.

When I reached for the tied belt at my waist, Graham gritted out, "*Pull yourself together, Penelope.*"

"Or what?" I asked.

He huffed. "Fine, look the fool you insist on acting like." We stood for half a minute, but it felt like an hour. His eyes softened and he reached for my elbow and for some reason, I let him. He leaned into me and kissed a cheek softly. "Goodbye, Penelope."

"Rot in hell, Graham Glenn." I smiled.

He left me with the last word, which wasn't as satisfying as I'd have liked.

When he walked out of sight, I crumpled onto the bottom step of a nearby row house as I cried into my hands. I heard a group of boys exiting Chelsea Potter and heading my direction. I pulled up my hose and buttoned my blouse to avoid unwanted attention, but it did no good. My pale skin, dark hair, and blue eyes invited their voices regardless.

"'Allo, love! Lookin' for a bit of company tonight?" one asked.

"No, thank you," I told them, running a hand through my hair as I attempted to avoid eye contact.

"Oh, come now, darlin'! I've a nice warm bed for one such as yourself," another teased. His friends laughed while I cringed.

"Lovely bird, sing us a song then!" a particularly drunk one rang out.

"Bit dodgy 'ere all on your lonesome, in-it?" the first boy who'd spoken asked.

More laughing.

"I'll keep ya safe, Yank. Come wit me then," a cockney accent promised.

"Shut it, David!"

Please, please, please, just walk on, boys.

I shook my head at them and buried my face in a veil of hair. It worked. Sort of.

They turned toward me as they passed and catcalled but eventually rounded the corner.

The little fraidy-cat adrenaline rush they gave me dried the tears. I bolted upright, desperate to get back to my flat. Well, my former flat. *Graham's* flat.

I walked back toward the pub to flag down a cabbie. A black cab swooped in for me and stuck his hand out of his window to open my door for me. I climbed in and he shut it behind me.

"Where to, love?" a middle-aged man with a giant mustache and even bigger smile asked.

"Robinson Street, please."

He shot forward and neither of us spoke for the short ride, which I was appreciative of.

As he approached our street, no, Graham's street, I leaned forward and placed my hand on the edge of his open partition window. "Number seven, please?"

He slowed down and noticed the state of the road. I cringed. "'Fraid you'll have to walk, love. No way of gettin in n' out there. Construction and all that."

"That's fine." I sighed, throwing a few pounds through the window and opening the door before he could get to it.

When I got out, the tears renewed tenfold. I found myself leaning against the wrought iron fences of a few terraced houses. *Just get home. Just get home*, I kept telling myself.

"It's not your home, though," I confessed to the wind, which brought on a whole new rush of tears.

Blubbering like a giant baby, I was too distracted by my pain to remember my neighbor's exposed sunken terrace garden, a ten-foot drop onto concrete.

Of course was all I remembered thinking as I tumbled down the rabbit hole.

Chapter
Three

I woke to the sounds of beeps and machines running. My eyes felt sluggish and difficult to open, so I decided I didn't want to and fell back asleep. The next thing I remember was a soft hand on my shoulder and a quiet voice at my ear.

"Dearie, can you hear me?" a woman asked. I felt another person busying around me, pulling at me from different places. I peeled my eyes open into slits, ignoring all my instincts to keep them closed. "The drugs make you sleepy, darling, I know, but try to wake up a little?"

I took a deep breath and forced my lids open to a little woman, dressed as a nurse, maybe early fifties, and a sweet smile. Another nurse, maybe a little older than I, was folding back a blanket from my lap. She smiled at me as she pushed a rolling tray to my bedside, a movement that came naturally to her, like she'd done it thousands of times. She wiped my forehead with a damp cloth.

"You took quite the tumble," the older woman told me. She was gathering little discarded pieces of what looked like cut-up tape of tiny styrofoam pillows lined five across.

I looked around me, noticing I was in a hospital, and remembering my fall into Graham's neighbor's sunken terrace.

"Oh my God," I said, still processing. I tried to bring my left hand to my face, but it felt heavy and ached badly, making me groan.

"Careful now," she said, bringing my casted, heavy arm back down to my side.

I followed the dizzy movement and noticed I also had a cast on my right leg.

"What happened?" I asked them.

They smiled at me, still busying themselves. The older nurse said, "You had two separate fractures in your leg." She pointed to my lower leg. "Both the tibia and the fibula, but they were clean enough to set. Your arm just had one compound fracture, which was set as well. They had to cast you past the elbow, though. They used a waterproof cast so you'll be able to shower and swim still. Just make sure that once you're done soaping up, you rinse the cast very well with clean water to prevent buildup."

"That can be a bit itchy," the younger nurse offered. "They set your arm in such a way that makes it easier to drain as well. You'll still need to come back next week for further X-rays to make sure they were all set well."

"I can't do that," I told her. "I have to get back to the States."

"You're not well enough to travel yet, sweetheart," she said, taking my vitals. She reached for a cup. "I'll need you to drink something. We can't release you until we know you can keep something down."

The older nurse bent over me and pushed strands of hair from my face. "Can you ring up a friend? You'll need someone to care for you for a few weeks, at least."

My eyes started to sting. "I don't have anyone like that here," I told her as I followed the other nurse's instructions and took a small sip of juice.

Her brows furrowed in pity. "I have to release you soon, love, but I'd feel better if I could hand you off to someone. Isn't there *anyone* you can call?"

Tears spilled over my cheeks. "My boyfriend broke up with me tonight, cheated on me. I really don't know anyone else here, not really."

The older nurse bit her lip in disapproval and shook her head.

"That's a right bastard move, that is," the younger nurse said.

"Louisa!"

The young nurse, Louisa, laughed. "It's true, in-it?"

"Yes, but compose yourself," the older nurse scolded. She turned toward me. "You've no other friends here?" she asked.

I thought for only a split second about calling Graham, but changed my mind just as quickly. "Th-there might be one person," I said.

I looked at the chair in my little emergency stall and asked Louisa for my phone. I'd texted Oliver when Graham was running late once. He'd asked me to do it because he knew Oliver wouldn't yell at me the way he would have had Graham called to make his excuses.

My finger hovered over Oliver Finn's name on my phone. I took a deep breath.

"Oliver is my ex's best friend," I told Louisa. "He doesn't like me much, but I think he's the only one of Graham's friends who would actually come to help me. The thought of talking to him is too terrible to imagine. Would you mind?" I asked her.

"Hand it over, sweetheart," she said, her hand out for the phone.

She smiled and took it from me. I watched as she pressed the face of the phone and brought it to her ear. My heart pounded then stopped cold when the expression on her face changed.

"'Allo, this Oliver?" Louisa asked. She rolled her eyes. "No, I'm not one of your birds from the pub." She grabbed my chart. "I'm calling on behalf of Penelope Beckett." She paused. "I don't know, but I'm calling from Chelsea and Westmins—" she said, but stopped.

She handed me the phone. "He hung up."

I sighed. "I figured as much," I told her.

"Sorry, babe," Louisa said, patting my hand. She picked up my casted arm and placed it on top of a pillow. "Rest up. In an hour, maybe two, when we think you're ready, I'll give you instructions on what to expect and how to care for yourself. For now, rest. Let the drugs wear off."

I nodded and laid my head back. I let sleep consume me, desperate to forget I was thousands of miles away from home, to forget my broken heart and broken bones, to forget my loneliness. *I just want to go home*, I thought as I drifted off to sleep.

Chapter
Four

When I woke, I tried to lift my arm, but the heavy weight dragged it right back down to the pillow it'd been resting on. I moaned in pain. The drugs had worn off.

"Well, well, well," I heard to my left.

Groggily, I turned. "*Oli?*" I asked.

"The one and only."

"What are you doing here?"

"Your nurse rang me."

I tried to sit up, but it didn't work. Oliver stood and hovered over me. "Let me find the bed's lift button." Soon I was elevated and sighed in relief. "Comfortable?" he asked.

"Yes, thank you."

He sat back and rested his elbows on the chair's arm rests. "Where's Graham?" he asked.

I smiled at him, unable to hide the tears.

"I'm one of the rest," I quoted from Oli's own words that night at the pub, the night I'd figured out Graham had met with Chloe for the first time.

Oli ran his hands through his hair. "Shit, Penny. I feel like an ass."

I laughed. "You *are* an ass," I told him, "but at least you're an ass who showed up." I felt my chin tremble. "Thank you, by the way."

"I was panicked when she told me you were here." He cleared his throat and ran his hands down the thighs of his jeans. "Thought something terrible had happened." His eyes met mine. "What did happen?"

I grinned at him. "Graham told me he found someone else. Said he left a few hundred pounds on our dresser for a flight back home. That I needed to be out by Monday."

Oli ran his hands down his face. "He's a twat," he explained.

"I know this. Well, I know this *now*. Actually, you told me he would do this, but I didn't believe you." I shrugged my good shoulder as if my whole world wasn't collapsing. "I believe you now."

He leaned forward, the back of an index finger wiped away a tear. "We're a sorry lot, Penny. You're too good for us."

I laughed. "I know."

He smiled and sat back down. "Who is it?"

I knew exactly the *who* he was asking about. "Chloe."

He nodded, like he knew who she was. I bit my lip to keep from sobbing. "Why didn't you warn me?"

His hands made fists at his knees. "Graham's my best mate, Penny."

I scoffed at this. "At the expense of what?" I asked. "Is loyalty more important than decency?"

"For men?" he asked.

"For *humans*," I countered.

"Listen, I've talked to the nurses," he said, changing the subject. "You'll need four weeks in the arm cast and six weeks in the leg."

"Doesn't matter. I only need you to grab that cash from Graham and my passport. I'm getting the hell out of this country and as far away from Graham as possible."

"Penny," he said. I looked at him. "You can't travel for several weeks. Can I at least call Graham? I mean, I think if he knew, he'd help you."

I shook my head. "You don't get it, Oli. I'd rather re-break these bones a thousand times before talking to him again. Besides, he wouldn't help me if you paid him a million pounds."

He gulped and averted his eyes.

"Oh shit," I breathed. "You've already called him."

"I had to!" he said defensively. "When I hung up on that nurse, I rang him up to see what had happened."

"Oli!" I yelled, making him jump.

"He's on his way."

"*Oh my God*. Oh my God. Help me. Help me," I said desperately, trying to edge myself into a sitting position. It was difficult and painful. "Help me out of this gosh damn bed right now, Oliver! I need out of here!"

"Calm down, Penny," he said, pressing my shoulders back until they rested against the hospital sheet. "Just talk to him."

"No," I insisted.

"Please, Penelope."

"Absolutely not," I told him, refusing to look at him.

"Penny," he begged.

My lower lip trembled. "It's like glass in a wound, Oli. Like lemon in a paper cut. I believe I've suffered enough, thank you. Don't force me into this kind of humiliation. You know Graham!" I whisper-yelled. "He'll gloat over this. *Please*, Oli," I asked, grasping his forearm with my good hand.

But it was too late. Graham leaned over the curtain, looking appropriately like the asshole I then knew he was. I dropped my grip on Oliver.

"Oh, Penelope," Graham offered with a feigned pout. It felt pitifully sarcastic, which hurt. "Were you *trying* to hurt yourself?"

I rested my head on the bed. "What fresh hell is this?"

I closed my eyes, refusing to look at him, but couldn't shut my ears. There weren't enough available hands.

"Let me take you home," Graham's posh accent rang through my ears.

"Over my dead body," I told him, a little bit of a forceful Texas twang popping out in my anger. My eyes opened then, but I kept them trained on the ceiling.

"You can stay with me for a few weeks at least," Graham proposed, as if he was being generous.

My eyes burned again, but I bit down, refusing him the satisfaction.

"No," I said with resolution.

"Penny," Oli soothed.

I dropped my head and looked Oliver dead in the eyes. "Oli, don't."

"Come on, he'll take care of you."

I took a deep breath through my nose. "Please don't make me go home with him. Please, Oli."

Oli wrapped his hands around his arms and turned his eyes from mine.

The nurse came in and explained everything to

Graham and Oliver on how to care for me. I would need to elevate my arm and leg for at least twenty-four hours to keep down the throbbing, but eventually I should start feeling pretty normal after that. They gave Graham a stack of discharge papers along with prescriptions and a map to a store that had more accessible medical gear, like a scooter for broken legs. In the meantime, Louisa gave me a crutch to hobble around on and a sling to bear the brunt of the weight of my arm cast.

They wheeled me out of the hospital in a wheelchair, and I waited for the cheating bastard who was my ex to pull up to the front. Oli stood next to me, but I refused to talk to him. When Graham pulled forward, I hobbled into the passenger seat. I'd been in the UK for eight months and I'd yet to get used to the flipped driver's seat.

Oli bent over the window, his muscular forearm resting against the top of the car. "Graham will take care of you, Penny."

I looked at him but didn't say a word. My lethargic arm slowly found the window button and I pulled up to shut him out. I stared out the windshield as Graham got in. Neither of us said a word as we meandered through streets to Graham's flat. When he parked, I refused his help getting out of the car. He called me a brat, but I wouldn't let him bait me. When we got to the front steps, though, I couldn't argue with his help because he pulled my crutch from underneath me and threw it at the top of the concrete stairs. He yanked me up—an arm underneath my knees, another around my back—and brought me into his flat, setting me down on his exceedingly uncomfortable couch because he refused to own any piece of furniture that didn't look modern and

29

therefore not worth sitting on.

He left the room without saying a word then returned and tossed a blanket and pillow at me.

"Good night, Penelope," he said coldly before shutting off the light.

I tucked the stiff, square sofa pillow behind my head and tried to get as comfortable as possible, which wasn't comfortable at all. My leg and arm throbbed something crazy. I wanted to punch Graham in the face.

"Chloe can have him," I told the empty room.

Chapter
Five

"Penny!" someone shouted, startling me awake.

"What!" I said, bolting upright. I groaned at the pain in my arm.

"Come on," Oliver said into the pitch-black room.

He flipped on the light, causing me to cover my throbbing face. My eyes adjusted to the brightness of the room and found him standing over me.

"What are you *doing*?" I asked him.

"I'm taking you to my flat," he said matter-of-factly.

"Why?" I asked him.

"I'm a daft asshole, apparently."

We heard Graham walking down the stairs. "What's going on?" he asked us.

"I'm taking her with me," Oli said.

Graham laughed, making my cheeks burn in embarrassment. "What for, mate?"

"Because you're a bit of a wanker, Graham, and for a minute there I thought you might do the right thing and care for her properly, so I decided to swing this way to see for myself."

"She's fine," Graham explained. "Right, Penelope?"

I opened my mouth to tell them both to go to hell, but Oli interrupted me. "I'll take her to my house."

He ran up the stairs and Graham followed. I could hear them arguing from where I lay.

"Did you even fill her prescriptions?" Oli asked Graham.

"Well, no, I thought I could do that in the morning."

"In the morning! You're taking the piss, man! She's probably hurting. And why is she on that damn couch?"

"I didn't think I could get her upstairs."

It got quiet, but I heard shuffling around the room.

"What are you doing, mate?" Graham asked Oliver.

"I'm taking it, Graham. I'll get her back home eventually."

I heard a *thud, thud, thud* until Oliver emerged from the stairs with my suitcase. "Be right back," he told me, leaving the flat, presumably toward his car. I heard the hatch of his car open and shut, then he emerged in the outline of the door.

"Come now," he said, yanking the blanket off my body. He picked me up much like Graham had earlier, but much more gently. He walked toward the door but turned with me in his arms toward my ex. "See you Friday," he said casually, as if he wasn't absconding Graham's flat with me. "Don't bring that girl or I might have to hit you," he added.

He turned and walked out the door. My eyes peered around one broad shoulder and watched Graham in his ridiculous robe and slippers. I shot up two fingers in a V, the English equivalent to flipping the bird then looked back up at Oli.

Thank you, I mouthed.

"Think nothing of it," he told me, placing me in the passenger seat of his car. "It was worth it just to be elbow deep in your skivvies for that minute," he teased.

My good hand went to my face as my cheeks flamed. He closed my door and rounded to the driver's side, settling in and hitting a button to start the engine of his Range Rover.

"How do you afford a car like this, Oli?" I asked, studying my surroundings.

"I work, Penny. Did you not think I worked?"

"Worked a room?" I joshed, but he didn't laugh. "Yes." I stared at him. "Honestly? I didn't much think of what you might do for a living."

"Well, I work from home so—"

"That's cushy."

"Guess so," he said, flipping on his blinker to indicate a turn.

The car was quiet.

"Thank you again," I told him.

He sighed as if he was annoyed but bit back a smile. "Stop. I won't have you apologizing every fifteen minutes. It'll go right to my head."

I genuinely smiled at him. "Your head couldn't afford it," I teased.

"You're so clever," he teased back.

"I'm not, though, am I?" He rolled his eyes at me. "How clever can a person be if they couldn't see what another actually warned them about?"

"Someone in love?" he asked.

"Maybe. Or maybe not. Being blinded by love is a characteristic for morons."

Oli laughed. "Shut it, Pen. Trusting your boyfriend is not moronic. It's endearing."

"Endearing, yes. And stupid."

"Come now, you," he said, pulling into a twenty-four-hour pharmacy to have my meds filled for me. "Don't turn bitter on me." He drove through the drive-thru and handed over the prescriptions along with my traveler's medical insurance and ID.

"Bitter is an ugly color on a woman," I agreed, "but there's one thing I never considered before."

"What's that?" he asked, driving off and parking in front when the pharmacist told us he needed half an hour to fill them.

"Most of those women never asked to wear it."

"Ah, with that I have to disagree."

"Why's that?" I asked.

"They have the option to choose."

"Nope. I guarantee it was flung upon them without their permission and no attempt at peeling it off will ever expose the sweet, trusting girl that once was underneath."

"Already you reek of it," he told me.

My mouth fell open. I ticked off each point on the fingers of one hand. "Graham cheated on me. Graham dumped me while I was tipsy and left me to walk home on my own. He left cash on our *shared* dresser like I am some sort of prostitute. When you told him I was in the hospital, he was a prick about taking me back, as if I was an inconvenience. And once I got home, he cruelly left me to fend for myself." Oliver's eyes were wide by the time I'd finished. I took two deep breaths and continued, "If that's not a recipe for justified bitterness, then I don't know what is."

"Point taken. I'm sorry on behalf of my friend."

I tried to smile. "Doesn't count, but the effort gets an A plus."

"My first ever," he told me, making me laugh.

"You weren't a good student?" I asked.

"Not even a bit. More interested in the extracurriculars, if you *catch* my drift," he told me, wagging his brows.

"I'll have nothing of yours that's catching, thank you."

"That was a burn if I've ever had one."

"Does it? Burn, that is?" I gestured toward his nether regions with a toss of my head.

He laughed wholeheartedly.

"You're brilliant," he told me, then sobered. "Maybe a little *too* brilliant."

"You always were fun to banter with, Oli," I told him.

There was a moment of silence before he said, "That made Graham mental, you know."

I looked at him, still feeling a little groggy from lack of sleep and the drugs. "What did? Our playful banter?"

"Yeah, that."

"Good then," I said, feeling a tiny bit of satisfaction from that knowledge.

Oli laughed. "I see you've moved past denial then."

"Skipped right through denial and went straight for anger," I told him.

"What's after anger?" he asked.

I repeated the five stages of grief for him. "Denial. Anger. Bargaining. Depression. Acceptance."

"He said girls who playfully fought were shameful," Oli added.

I couldn't help it, I laughed harder than necessary. "He's such a prick."

Oli laughed along with me. "I know," he agreed.

I wiped tears of laughter away. "Then why be his friend?"

"I've known him since we were kids, Penny. He's loyal to me."

"That you know of," I told him.

"Say what you want about him, but the one thing Graham has going for him is his loyalty to his mates."

"To a fault then."

"Yes," Oli agreed, "even to a fault."

I narrowed my eyes at him. "That's so," I paused, "*faithful,*" I dug at him.

He didn't respond.

"Tell me something," I prodded. "What do you wonder he thinks of your helping me now?"

Oliver wrapped his hands around his arms. "Not sure."

I let that sit. "Do you remember the night Graham and I met?"

"Yes, I do. It was raining. We were at the W in Dallas. You were a cocktail waitress."

"Wow, can't believe you remember that."

"I remember because I wanted to try you on, but Graham called dibs."

Oli expected me to laugh, but I couldn't get past the shock of his admission. "You *did*?" I asked. I shook my head to clear my thoughts. "You want to try every girl on, though."

"I'm a bit more selective than that," he explained. "Anyway, Graham never called dibs on a girl I was interested in, so I let him go for it."

"I'm such gullible girl," I told him.

"Graham is a better consequence compared to yours truly."

"Not so sure about that. Look at the pain it's caused."

"But then you wouldn't be here now," Oli told me, as if that would have been a terrible thing. But it was. It really was.

"*Exactly.*"

Oli looked a little taken aback by what I'd said. "You and I would have remained friends regardless if Graham had taken me home with him or not," I told him.

"Oh yeah? How do you figure that?"

"By the end of your visit, I'd spent enough time with you all to warrant a regular phone call."

Oli shrugged his shoulders and nodded in approval.

"You want to hear something funny?" I asked him.

"Go on then."

"I hated Graham hanging out with you these past few months."

He looked mock hurt. "*Me?*"

"Yes, I thought you were a bad influence," I admitted.

"Ha!" Oli ribbed with a wink.

"I know." I stared out the window. A light rain had begun to fall and it turned the pavement into reflections of the neon lights surrounding us. "What a fool I've been."

"*Love looks not with the eyes, but with the mind. And therefore is winged Cupid painted blind,*" Oli beautifully recited.

"What's that mean, Oliver?"

"That when one falls in love with another, you see them as you want to see them. All you can see is the good that attracted you in the first place. You are blind to their faults."

"Color me winged Cupid painted blind, then."

"Come on, Cupid," he said, starting the car again. "Let's get your meds."

We went through the line and he paid for my medications. "Thank you for that," I told him. "I can make a wire transfer to you if I can get to my computer."

"Hush, think nothing of it."

"Well, thank you."

"I told you," he said, pulling out of the "car park" as they call it. "Those thank yous will go straight to my head."

I smiled a watery smile at him. "Thank you, Oli."

He surprised me by blushing a little. "Penelope Beckett, I've asked you repeatedly to *haud yer wheesht*!"

"Okay, you got it," I told him, giggling.

A few minutes later we pulled into an underground garage below a very old-looking building on Brewery Square. "Holy cannoli, Oli! Do you live here?"

"Yes, Penny, I live here."

"Which floor?" I asked.

"All of them," he answered as if he didn't just gesture toward several million pounds' worth of house.

I laughed. "Are you rich, Oli?"

"Not really. This is my family's estate. I just technically care for it," he explained.

"That's kind of cool," I said, thinking about my parents' "estate" back home, a cookie cutter in the suburbs of Dallas.

"It's nice not having to pay rent, so yeah, I guess you could say it's cool."

"Yes," I mocked him in a bad English accent, "I suppose it is satisfactory, Lady Penelope. One lump or two, darling?"

"Come on, clever girl," he said, after opening my door and lifting me from his car. He grunted.

"Hey!" I complained. "The casts add at least twenty pounds. Maybe thirty or forty. Possibly fifty," I added when he had to lift me up a few steps to a metal door.

He laughed. "You weigh hardly anything, you daft girl. It's just a bit awkward is all."

We stepped through an old room with two fireplaces. It looked like a long mudroom to me, but it had dark wood plank flooring and dark stone walls. The tall, ancient-looking windows that lined one wall held the only light coming from the streetlamps outside. He set me down on a leather chesterfield sofa draped with some sort of white fur blanket.

"Don't get too comfortable," he said. "I'm only going for your things. I've got an extra room on the first floor here I think you'll like."

"Okay, Oli," I said, studying my surroundings.

Against the wall perpendicular to the windows and near the metal door entrance was an incredibly large wood antique cabinet and worktable. On top of the desk rested all sorts of strange tools I wasn't familiar with and scraps of the finest leather I'd ever seen strewn about. An old but comfortable-looking chair waited in front of the desk. It was so well worn it almost looked lonely for its regular owner. I wondered if that owner was Oli.

When Oli returned with my bag and my medicine, he

locked the door behind him and faced me. Suddenly our usual playful banter felt too familiar to practice in that room, in what was Oliver Finn's home. Banter was a cover for us. It was what we did because neither of us had any intention of ever becoming more than general acquaintances who only chatted up seriously twice a year.

How are the kids, yeah? he would have asked in ten years.

Great, Oli, they're great. Growing like weeds.

That's brilliant, Penny. Give my love to Graham.

In all the scenarios I'd ever imagined, Graham and I were married. My whole body felt inexplicably heavy.

"I'm pretty tired, Oliver," I told him.

He started and quickly moved forward, shuffling my stuff into a room that jutted off the one he'd sat me in. He came back and picked me up, finally showing me the mystery room he'd promised.

"Uh, this is beautiful," I stated, but it was restrained.

The room was glorious. A nice big bed with antique frame and a fluffy, comfortable duvet over a plethora of overstuffed pillows. There was a crystal chandelier that hung from the ten-foot plaster ceiling. On the cream-painted brick walls hung original art I would have guessed were probably worth more than my life.

"Thank you," he said, placing me on the bed.

I sank into the soft textures like a stone in the sea. I held back the sigh that rose to my throat. Never had I ever laid in such a comfortable bed.

"Uh, Oli?" I asked.

"Yes?"

"Could I bother you for a shower?" I asked, pulling out of my hair pieces of grass I'd gotten when I'd fallen.

"Right. A shower."

He lifted me back up and brought me through what I decided to call the workshop room and into a spacious kitchen with a large island in the center, then into another bedroom attached to a small hall. The bedroom was lovely but not as nice as the one he'd picked out for me. The bathroom, however, was something I'd only ever seen on television.

"Wow!" I said, taking in the galley bathroom. At the end was a sunken, jetted tub. The modern look was so different from the age of the home, but somehow it fit.

The tub called my name, but for the sake of saving time, I opted for the open shower with the spout settled in the ceiling above the tub.

"Okay, how do we do this?" he asked.

My cheeks burned. "Uh, well, maybe just unbutton my blouse for me. They ripped the sleeve, so maybe you can just tear the rest off? I have a little cami underneath and I'll just have to wrestle that off myself, I guess. Do that, then unzip my skirt. That's easily removed, at least. I think I can get the rest."

"Okay," he said. I watched as his slender fingers undid the buttons of my blouse then tugged at the cut fabric at my shoulder and ripped off the rest of my shirt. When he laid the ruined garment aside, he unzipped my skirt.

He stood back, keeping his eyes on the tile floor. "I'll leave you to it then," he said as he backed out of the room.

I began to pull my camisole up when he darted back in. "Sorry! Sorry, forgot to show you a few things. Here's a towel and a robe for you," he said, pulling those out of a discreet linen closet I hadn't really seen when I'd first walked in. "There's shampoo and conditioner next to the tub, shower scrub, and all that. Uh, yeah, just shout if you need anything."

I smiled and nodded as he he left the room. I struggled for at least ten minutes to get fully undressed and somehow hobbled to the shower and turned it on. I let the water warm up then sat beneath the spray for several minutes before attempting to wash my hair with one hand.

"This is going to get annoying," I told no one.

I washed my body then let the clean water run through my casts fully, like the nurse said, to make sure I wasn't leaving any suds. I turned the water off and let them drain well. I dried myself, awkwardly threw my wet hair into the towel, and wrapped the robe around my body.

I tried to lift myself out of the tub, but it wasn't happening.

"Um, Oli!" I called out tentatively. "Oli!" I shouted.

"Yeah?" he answered.

"I can't climb out of your tub."

"I didn't even think about that," he said. "Can I come in?" he said from around the open wall.

"Yes, come in," I told him, trying to cinch the robe a little tighter. It was hard with only hand.

Oli came in. "You look very fetching," he teased.

"Yeah, yeah," I told him. "Do me a solid?"

"What do you need?"

"Without exposing me, can you tie this robe tighter for me?"

He laughed and reached down to help me. "I'm usually loosening this belt, not tightening it."

"Well, not this time, bucko." He pulled the belt tighter

for me.

"How's that then?"

"Better," I told him.

He lifted me up and carried me back to his guest room. He laid me across the bed again and reached for my bag for me. "What do you want to wear?" he asked.

He rummaged through my things, which thoroughly irritated me, but I couldn't complain, not after his kindness.

"Just give me those," I told him, pointing to a pair of plain black panties. I was mortified when he handed them over with a teasing smile. "Shut it," I ordered.

"I never said a thing."

"But you were thinking it!"

"What else?" he asked.

"Those," I said, pointing to a pair of green pajama shorts I thought might be big enough for my leg cast to fit through. "And that," I said, pointing to a white tank top.

He handed them both over. "Fair warning?" he asked.

"Huh?"

"I'm just warning you that this house is old and with that *charm* comes poor insulation. It gets rather chilly in here at night."

I looked at the down comforter. "I think I'll be okay," I told him.

"Fine then. Call me when you're dressed," he said, leaving and shutting the door behind him.

I struggled for another twenty minutes with an act that should have only taken thirty seconds tops. I'd forgotten to ask for a sports bra, so I had to get one on my own, which was a feat, let me tell you.

When all was said and done, I'd worked up quite a

sweat and didn't have any fear of getting cold throughout the night.

"Okay, Oli!" I said. He came back in quickly.

I decided he must have been in his workshop. Whether he was waiting or working, though, I didn't know.

"You rang, milady?"

"Yes, I'm ready to be tucked in."

He laughed, reaching forward with a few pills and a glass of water. I took them, set the water aside, and let him put me in bed. He piled up a bunch of pillows and rested my leg cast on top. I almost moaned in relief. He pulled the covers over me, except around my broken leg, and it felt like such an intimate thing to do, I blushed.

"Good night, *Penny* & Joon."

"Hardy har har. Good night, Oliver & Company."

"Hardy har har," he mocked.

He shut off the lights and closed the door behind him.

And that's when the loneliness set in.

My good hand went to what was Graham's side of the bed and I cried quietly into the mountain of Oliver's pillows.

I made a mistake, I told myself. *A mistake that is going to cost me something greater than I think I have.*

"Damn you, Graham Glenn," I whispered.

Chapter
Six

I woke early, too early. Like, the-morning-sun-had-yet-to-rise kind of early. I sighed and lifted my arm to test the weight.

"Oh my gato, this is a pain in the ass."

I tried to lift my leg, but it trembled with the effort. *Note to self: stay fit, so a pathetic attempt at lifting a simple lower leg cast won't make you feel like a complete failure.* Who was I kidding? Working out was for suckers. Not really, though. Diabetes is no joke. Those poor people don't eat sugar!

I swung the leg over the edge of the bed and sucked in a quick breath when my thigh muscle couldn't hold the brunt of the weight. I bit my bottom lip to keep from shouting in pain and waking Oliver. Nope, working out is definitely *not* for suckers.

Oli had laid my crutches against the wall near the bed, so I reached for them. I took a deep breath as I grappled to right myself and stay upright. I was going to need to practice that move, I could tell. I hobbled over to my bag and searched for the blow-dryer and curling iron I had to buy when I got to the UK. Converter plugs didn't work. Trust me. American blow-dryers required more electricity than English outlets were willing to give. I learned that the hard way when I blew out one of Graham's sockets. That was the first time I'd ever been introduced to his passive-aggressive ways. It was a cold day in that house that day, let me tell ya.

I carefully balanced on my good leg and reached with my good hand for my hair. It was thick and I'd never actually had it dry overnight when I slept on it. So it was still damp, of course, and it gave me that humid-icky feeling. I threw the dryer and my curling iron with my bag of alligator clips onto the bed then reached for my laptop.

Sliding my foot with the broken leg across the floor, I stumbled back toward the bed and carefully laid my computer on the duvet before balancing the crutches against the wall as Oli had and sliding back into bed.

I wanted to yell at the top of my lungs at how frustrating the whole process was. What would have taken a minute usually took me at least five. I was moving at a snail's pace and for someone who was impatient, it was like water torture.

I pried open my laptop and tried to log in to my blog but realized I didn't know Oli's Wi-Fi password. I ran a beauty blog back in the States that had gained popularity. I had more than three million subscribers on YouTube along with several social media accounts. It was nice because I was able to gain some monthly income from the advertising revenues I received. All in all, I made an average of about three thousand dollars a month. It wasn't anything to write home about since my exorbitant school loans ate up about a third of that (did you know they expect you to pay that crap back?). I'd only been doing it for two years and it allowed me some independence in the United Kingdom. I didn't really require a work visa and because I could prove that I could afford to support myself, I received a permanent visa fairly easily.

I thought back to the day that I'd received the visa and felt the ire of that morning come seeping back into my pores. Graham, shocked apparently, asked why I'd applied for the visa without discussing it with him first. I asked him what the big deal was if were going to be together forever. He told me I was a little high handed since we'd never talked about it. Another red flag I totally missed.

I was constantly looking for new things to vlog, so I decided there wasn't a better tutorial than one of me trying to do my hair and makeup while in a cast. I couldn't find anything similar online on my phone and thought it would get me a lot of views, especially when I explained the story behind it. I didn't hold back with my followers. They knew everything that was going on in my life, much to Graham's dismay.

I played with several techniques on how to do my hair and pinpointed an easy one that seemed the most efficient. I shuffled to the light switch in the room and flipped on the light. I set to rights all my filming lighting and my camera equipment at the desk on the wall opposite the bed and sat down with my blow-dryer and curling iron. I filmed my B-roll first, which was essentially me doing my hair from beginning to end. It was exhausting. When I edited all the footage, the B-roll would be fast-forwarded so my poor viewers wouldn't be subject to all my cursing. Plus, instant gratification! Yaay!

When I had all my curls in alligator clips on top of my head, I stood and almost fell over. I decided I'd leave that footage in for kicks and reached for my makeup bag. I filmed myself doing my makeup with one hand but talked throughout the process. I could fast-forward whatever parts needed speeding up later.

I cut a different roll after my makeup was done, but while my hair cooled so it would set, about what had happened to me. I was so proud of myself for not crying and ruining my makeup. I would cut that in at the beginning so viewers wouldn't be confused. Then I pulled all the alligator clips from my hair and shook out the curls, turning my head over and spraying them so they'd hold, before flipping my head back over and spritzing a few curls in the front.

All in all it was a dramatic look and would make for a dramatic vlog. I hoped it'd get a ton of views. Whenever that happened, I always got a few more advertisers, which would pad my pocket a little more.

I painstakingly edited my video, setting it to a few stock music pieces I used regularly, and set up my newest blog to publish when I had Internet connection then shut my laptop. I peered down at my phone. It was seven thirty in the morning and I'd already done a full day's work. My arm ached. I stood up, gathered my crutches, and staggered out of the guest room in search of more pain pills.

I was shocked still when I caught Oli in the corner, sitting in that old worn chair next to the huge antique worktable and cabinet. He was engrossed in something.

"Good morning, chatterbox," he greeted without lifting his head.

I limped his direction. "Oh my God, did I wake you?" I asked him.

I saw the corner of his mouth raise. "No, you did not. You can't hear anything in that room unless you're in here." His bright green eyes finally met mine and it startled me a bit. His dark, longish hair was disheveled on top of his head, like he'd rolled out of bed and didn't bother running a brush through it, but it looked fantastic. Boys were an unfair lot.

"Well, look at you," he continued. His hands held a tool and a bit of leather in them. He let them fall into his lap. "Your hair is down."

I felt my good hand run self-consciously through a few curls. "Uh, yeah, I was filming a new segment for my vlog and, honestly, this is how I usually wear my hair."

"I know. I remember," he said, remarking on our Dallas days and busying his hands. They stilled again, as if he remembered something else. He stood and pushed a big comfortable chair next to his workstation for me to sit in. He helped me down into it and I breathed a sigh of relief. "More pain pills?" he asked.

"Yes, please."

He sprinted for the kitchen, which I thought was endearing. He returned with two more pills and another glass of water. I took them from him, downing the pills and handing back an empty glass.

"Are you hungry?" he asked. "You should probably take a bit of food with those."

"Uh, sure," I told him. "Are you hungry?"

"I'm a guy. I'm always hungry." He stretched his hands over his head and the movement pulled up the hem of his T-shirt. "Stay here, Pen."

"Like I could go anywhere," I sarcastically bit out.

I could hear him laughing all the way into his kitchen. I heard pans shuffling around and a burner light on his stove, then something sizzling in a pan. He returned fifteen minutes later with a plate of eggs and sausage.

"Wow, this looks incredible," I said as my stomach rumbled, making me laugh.

He handed me my plate and sat in his chair with his. We ate in silence for a few minutes, but my curiosity ate at me as well, so I asked, "What is all this?" I gestured toward his workbench and all the tools.

Oliver's brows furrowed. "Graham never told you what I did?"

"No, actually."

He shook his head as if he was annoyed with his friend. "I'm a master leatherworker."

I couldn't stop the laugh that bubbled up from my throat. "*What?*" I asked in disbelief.

He smiled at me. "It's a family business handed down through the generations for over five hundred years."

I coughed on my eggs. Oli patted my back to help things along. When I gained composure again, I shouted, "Five hundred years!"

"Yes, madam, that is correct."

"You are pulling my leg," I told him.

"That would probably hurt," he teased.

I studied him with my mouth agape.

"What is so hard to believe about this?" he asked me.

I looked at the top of his bench at all his ancient-looking tools. "I guess it's not that difficult to imagine now that I'm sitting here with you and this monstrosity of a cabinet full of crazy tools and scraps of patinated leather everywhere. I'm just a little confused. What do you make?"

"My family has made all equestrian leather bags for the royal family for five hundred years. They've had a standing account with us for that long, and the trade was handed down father to son and so on, keeping the art alive."

I was dumbfounded. "That is fascinating, Oliver."

He sat his empty plate on the bench next to him and fell into his chair. "I suppose it is."

"Suppose away, Oli." I looked at him in a different light. "Do you only make bags for the royal family?"

"No, I sell bags all over the world."

He stood up, disappearing into another room and returned with one of the most beautiful leather bags I'd ever seen. Somewhere between leaving for the bag and retrieving it, he'd put on white cloth gloves.

"Is that to protect the leather?" I asked, pointing to a gloved hand.

"Yeah."

"What do you charge for one of these?" I asked.

He barked a laugh. "A lot."

I smiled at him. "Thus the Range Rover."

He nodded. "Thus the Range Rover."

I made him turn the bag over so I could check it out from all angles. I was growing more and more impressed by the minute. "Are these bags the only thing you make?" I asked him.

"No," he said, "but this one and other equestrian

goods are the only things I sell."

"What do you mean?"

"I make all kinds of things, but no one wants them. They only want the bags the royal family buys."

"Let me see what else you make," I asked.

He stood taller, looking down at me, his head cocked to one side. "You *really* want to see them?"

"Uh, *duh*."

"Penny the Eloquent, as always," he needled.

"Shut up and get the other stuff."

"Fine," he said, retreating from the room once more.

He emerged with a plethora of things, but immediately my eyes went to a single handbag hanging on a few fingers on his left hand.

"That!" I exclaimed, pointing to it.

"My sister designed it," he told me, holding the bag in front of my face.

My fingers itched to touch it. "It's like a cross between a Birkin and a hobo or something."

"I have no clue what that means." He snorted. "She only told me what she wanted and I made it."

"It's brilliant, Oli," I told him, sincere.

"Really?" he said, looking at it as if he'd only just noticed the most finely crafted bag ever known to man, a bag *he* created.

I studied the stitch work, how pliable the patinated leather was, the color, the shape, how well it hung in his hand. "Oli," I whispered with reverence, "this is art, dude."

He laughed at me and shook his head, then turned to put up all the pieces he'd brought in.

"I didn't even really get to see the other stuff!" I yelled.

"Another time, Penny."

"Fine," I said, before I remembered I needed his Wi-Fi password. "Hey!" I called out.

"What do you need?"

"I need your Wi-Fi password. I've got to upload this vlog."

He came back in the room then cut across to mine, bringing my laptop back with him and opening the lid.

"You mind?" he asked.

"Not at all," I answered.

He typed in his password for me and turned the computer my direction.

"Hit publish?" he asked, the little pointer hovering over the button.

"Hit it." He did. "Now go to the YouTube tab already opened."

"Okay."

"Upload that file there," I told him, pointing at my recent vid.

When he was done with that, I asked him to go to the social media platform I uploaded from and he did, typing out my status and attaching the new video.

"Bugger me," he said when it was all said and done.

I laughed. "It's tedious work," I told him.

"No shit."

"Well, it makes me money."

He studied me. "Pretty innovative," he complimented. This surprised me, and I guessed my face showed it if his reaction was any indication. "What?" he asked.

"You just paid me a compliment, Oli."

"So I did. I'm not quite the heartless bastard you make me out to be."

My eyes narrowed. "You think I think you're a heartless bastard?"

He coughed into a hand and turned toward his bench, picking up a tool and a piece of leather. "Don't you?"

"Not at all," I said. "I just think you sell yourself short is all. I told Graham I thought something happened to you that made you act the way you did."

His head whipped toward me. "*What?*" he asked, his chest pumping air.

What is this?

"Nothing, nothing," I said, "Never mind. Just a passing thought."

His breathing slowed as he returned to his work. I picked up my laptop and checked all my social media accounts. I turned the monitor toward Oliver and pointed to the number of views the video on my YouTube account had already gotten.

"Holy shit!" he exclaimed. "Over three thousand views!"

"I know! It always blows me away. It never gets old."

He reached over and hit the play button. Only a little self-conscious, I considered him as he watched the video.

When it was over, he looked at me. "Did you edit that?" he asked.

"Yeah. I've found when you do twice-weekly vids, though, that the editing part gets easier and easier as you practice. You know how to produce the footage more efficiently for optimal editing purposes and all that glorious stuff."

"It's amazing, actually."

I felt my cheeks tinge pink. "Thank you."

"Yet *another* thank you!"

I laughed then shut down the computer, setting it to the side. "When do you think you'll be finished up here?" I asked.

"I can be done whenever I want. Perks of owning your own business and all that."

"I just wanted to run over to that medical supply store the nurse told us about. I don't think I can hobble around on these crutches for much longer."

Oli picked up his phone and checked the time. "It's probably open now. What do you say? Should we go?"

"Yeah, just let me brush my teeth, will you?"

"Here," he said, lifting me up easily. It gave me a little head rush.

He carried me into his kitchen and sat me on top of his island, next to the most charming farm sink I'd ever seen. He left and returned with my toothbrush and toothpaste. He cleaned up his kitchen while I brushed my teeth.

He helped me find an outfit that would fit around my casts. It wasn't the most flattering ensemble, but there was nothing I could do about that. I updated my social stuff by taking a goofy picture and letting everyone know where I was headed. We hit the road in less than half an hour and drove toward the supply store. We drove around the city block the store sat on a few times, waiting for a parking spot.

"There!" I yelled when I saw a little Ford backing up out of its space. Oli gunned it and put on his blinker.

"You're an excellent parking space spotter."

"Just one of my many qualities," I bragged, pretending to wipe imaginary dust from my shoulder.

We parked and he dragged me out of the car, setting

me down then handing me my crutches. I hitched myself up the curb with only one slight stumble. I was improving.

The store was full of all kinds of strange things. They had something that literally looked like a metal peg leg. You just bent your leg at the knee and strapped it to your leg. You could adjust it to your height. It looked handy, but I couldn't justify spending three hundred pounds for something I was only going to need for a few weeks. I opted for the scooter. It was only eighty pounds. I rode it around the store, then Oli found another, and I giggled when he joined me. I don't think the store's owners were all that happy with us, but they said nothing.

I bought the scooter and a couple of other little things a store employee claimed would help me during my recovery. As I rode the scooter out of the store, I felt a little bit more independent, which was soothing. I wasn't moving as slow as molasses anymore, and that was all I really wanted.

"Happier?" Oliver asked.

"Yes," I told him.

And I was. In that moment, anyway, because I'd been distracted. But everyone knows when you are at your lowest, it's the nature of the beast to kick you while you're down. Everyone knows that. Apparently I'd forgotten, though.

I smiled up at Oli, but his own had fallen. He shuffled back and forth on his feet, deciding something. "What's wrong?" I asked.

"Shit, Penny, I'm sorry," he said, but before I could ask him what was up, I heard Graham's voice to my right.

"Oliver. Penelope," he said with little inflection.

I turned toward him, followed the line of his face, down his shoulder, arm, to his hand intertwined with another's. I forced my gaze up to look at her.

"Why?" Oliver asked him, his hands open in disbelief.

I looked up at Oli. "Because he wanted me to see him. With her."

Graham tried to hide a smile. "That's sick," Oli commented.

I turned toward Chloe. I was several inches taller than her, but what she lacked in height, she made up for in chest and hips. "Do you remember me?" I asked her.

"*Oui*," she answered in French.

I compared her lilting accent to my slight twang in my head and felt my cheeks heat. I'd planned on laying into them, but lost confidence immediately. Graham stood before me, well put together as always. Chloe stood next to him with her designer clothing and shoes. She fit on his arm so well it made me feel ill. I peered down at my casted arm and leg, at my baggy pants and T-shirt. My *scooter*.

I cleared my throat. "Well, should we get going, Oli?" I asked him.

He looked down on me with pity. I hated it. So much. I looked toward the ground. "We've got a lot to do today," he told our arsehole sidewalk patrons and led me toward his car.

He lifted me into his arms and whispered in my ear. "Keep it together for just a little longer," he ordered.

I bit my trembling lip and nodded when he sat me in his car. I stared straight ahead while he loaded all my stupid medical supply stuff in the back.

When he got in, he started the car and backed up. At

the intersection, we stopped at a stoplight and he checked his rearview mirror.

"Okay," he said.

All the pain, anger, and fury that'd welled up in my body came flooding out in a desperate sob. I buried my face into my good hand.

"I'm so sorry," Oliver said at my right. "I'm so sorry."

I bellowed into my hand, unable to control myself. In the back of my mind I knew I was going to be mortified later, but in the moment couldn't seem to grasp that enough to compose myself. Instead, I wept harder than I ever had in my entire life.

I don't even remember driving into Oliver's garage. He ran to my side and lifted me. I wrapped my arm around his neck and grieved into his shoulder.

"It really hurts," I told him.

"I'm so sorry. Do you need another pain pill?"

"No," I confessed. "Here," I said, pushing my fingers into my chest. "Right here. Like an elephant is resting right here and no amount of pushing will get him off."

"I'm so sorry," Oliver kept repeating.

He took me back to my room and laid me down on the bed. He elevated my arm and leg then hovered over me for a moment. He ran off somewhere and returned with a warm, damp washcloth. He softly wiped my face then set it aside.

"I'm so sorry," he soothed over and over. After a while, I decided he wasn't even aware he was saying it.

His palm found my chest, where the pressure was overwhelming, and as if he was somehow familiar with its exact place, he pressed lightly. I closed my eyes at the relief it gave me. I wrapped my good hand around his wrist to keep it there. I breathed freely; my lungs no longer burned.

I opened my eyes, blurry from the salt of my tears. "Thank you."

"You're welcome," he whispered, lifting his hand.

He crawled into the bed and laid beside me.

"You're wondering how I know that tortured point," his deep voice said, interrupting the quiet.

"Yes," I replied.

"You were right. When you told him that you suspected I acted the way I did because something had happened to me? You were right."

"I see."

Oli turned toward me and kissed my temple, not ready to admit more. "Try to sleep. That's the only thing that will help in the beginning like this."

"Okay," I said, my whole body feeling numb.

I expected him to leave, but he didn't and I was so grateful. We both laid staring up at the ceiling and before I knew it, somehow my lids began to droop.

"Thank you," I whispered.

Chapter
Seven

When I woke, the daylight streaming through the
windows disoriented me. I turned to my right, half
expecting to see Graham, but saw Oliver's dark head
instead. I fought back the tears then remembered
Graham's smug face on the sidewalk with Chloe's hand
inside his and they dried quickly.

My blood boiled in my veins. Trying not to wake
Oliver, I carefully lifted myself off the bed, but was
startled still when Oli grabbed my wrist.

"What are you doing, silly girl?"

I looked at him over my shoulder. "I didn't want to
wake you."

"Here," he said, standing and wiping the sleep from
his eyes. "Stay there. Let me get the scooter from the car
for you."

I nodded and he bounded down the small step at the
door of my room into the workroom. I listened for the
metal door. A few minutes later, he set the scooter in front
of my room, then hopped up, coming to my side and

lifting me.

"Getting used to the weight by now, are you?" I teased.

"Enough of that, Penelope."

I smiled at him as he set me at my scooter. I hopped on and rolled behind him into the kitchen. I grinned because I could keep up with him.

"What's so funny?" he asked.

I shook my head. "Nothing, really. I just don't like being a burden, so my being able to nip at your heels like this makes me a little giddy."

He barked a laugh. "It's the little things."

I nodded sarcastically. "It really is."

"Are you hungry?" he asked.

"Starvin' Marvin."

I sat on the edge of my scooter while he worked at making a pesto pasta with salad. I brought my phone to my face to check the status of my latest vlog.

"Holy shit, Oli!" I shouted.

"What?" he yelled, spilling pesto on the counter.

"Sorry," I told him, biting my lip to keep from laughing.

"It's fine," he said, mopping it up into the sink. "What's going on?"

"My latest vlog. It has over a million views already."

Oliver's mouth dropped open in disbelief. "I know!" I yelled.

"It's the story," he said.

"The breakup or the fall?"

"Both," he said, returning to his sauce.

"Well, hopefully Revlon calls, baby."

He smiled. "I hope so too."

"I think my next vid will be on how to look stylish while still sporting these things," I said, lifting my leg and arm casts.

Oli snorted.

"Mock all you want, but this is how I make that cold hard cash."

"I'm not mocking." He laughed.

"Sure you aren't."

"After dinner," he said casually, "would you like to sit with me in the workroom? I can show you how I make my bags."

"That would be cool. Maybe, if you have time this week, since I'll just be sitting around here, you can show me how to make one of those handbags too?"

I rocked the scooter back and forth with my good foot, unable to sit still.

"That's a sixty-hour bag, easily."

"Sixty hours? Dang, dude!"

"What? You don't have sixty hours to spare?"

I waved him away. "I do. You know I do."

"Then, as you say, *chill*."

I gut laughed at his attempt at my American accent.

"Do I not pull it off?" he asked.

I shook my head.

Oliver and I sat down to dinner. Afterward I tried to help him clean up, but I was lousy at it with only one hand. It exasperated him because he said he couldn't focus, too afraid I might fall and he'd have to stand behind me to catch me. He forced me to sit back down on my scooter while he finished up.

When he was done, he set me on his leather chesterfield and propped up my leg and arm on pillows and turned the couch so I could get a better view of him working. I watched as he placed a worn leather apron around his neck but didn't tie the strings around his waist.

"You can only stab yourself in the thigh so many times before this becomes habit," he explained.

"Do you stab yourself often?"

"Haven't done that for ages, but it's one of those crutches I still hold on to."

He sat down, one booted foot rested against the bottom of the workbench. The way he sat was second nature to him. I could tell he barely thought of it anymore. He grasped at his tools with his strong hands and his long fingers with such authority it was sort of thrilling to be witness to what I could tell was going to be something magical.

He stuck his phone into a speaker pod and hit play on his music app. Dark acoustic guitar rang out and it set such a heavy tone, something I didn't think he was even aware of. With casual confidence he picked up an equestrian bag I wasn't familiar with the name of and worked steadily and with such an assured manner, I was convinced he was making it look much easier than it actually was.

He matched two similar pieces of leather together, painstakingly examining their edges. He set the pieces down on the bench then pulled at a long strand of linen twine and cut it off from the spool set in the bench. He ran the twine through a block of beeswax over and over until he felt it was ready. He set the matched pieces between a wood clamp he kept in his lap that looked easily two hundred years old. With one tool, he punched holes into the seam of the two pieces of patinated leather then threaded the waxed twine through. He did this over and over with the precision of a machine.

"Do you mark where you need to punch the holes?" I asked after a few minutes of him working silently. I, rapt with interest.

"No," he answered, not looking away from his work. "Eventually I got good enough I didn't need to do that. It took years, really, to perfect this technique."

"How long did you train?" I asked.

His head down, he said, "I started working with Dad and Granddad when I was around thirteen, I guess. I made my first completed bag that actually sold to a duke when I was seventeen, though."

"That's fascinating," I told him. "Did you know you wanted to do this even at thirteen?"

His eyes broke from the bag as he looked at me. "I can't imagine doing anything else," he told me.

I smiled at him and he returned to what he was doing. When he was done stitching, he took out a small metal hammer and set the newly created seam carefully. During the next two hours, Oli pulled out several different and strange tools, working diligently. I kept up a barrage of questions, but he was patient while answering all of them, which upset me a little bit. Not because I was a masochist, but because Graham would have never stood for that. He would have shut me up with a passive-aggressive insult. It was yet another reminder I had been such a fool for Graham.

I studied the floor, thinking of how much I hated him and yet loved him so painfully. It wasn't fair you could know those two emotions together, both for one person.

"Uh-oh," I heard at my left.

My head rose. "What's that?"

"You're sad. I can tell you're getting gloomy."

"I'm sad, yes, but I'm also bloody pissed. I'm more angry than anything else."

"I know that feeling well," he told me.

I counted to three in my head. "Can you talk about it?" I asked him.

He set down his tools and the bag he was working with on the bench. He reached for something underneath his workbench. Carefully, he placed the bag in a velvet case and set it aside then put the tools in all their rightful places as well as hanging his leather apron on a hook on the wall. I wasn't expecting him to answer, but after ten minutes, he surprised me when he did.

He closed up his large cabinet and sat back down, facing me. "What has Graham told you about me?"

My eyes went to the top of my head as if I could read the memory. "Honestly? Nothing," I told him, embarrassed for Graham, as if I should be embarrassed for him. *The bastard.*

Oli nodded like he'd expected my answer. He unconsciously gripped the armrests of his chair and took one solid breath before meeting my gaze. "I was married once," he stated without emotion.

My mouth went dry. "*Married?*"

He grinned something caustic. "Yes, I fell madly in love once. I was twenty-two. She was beautiful," he explained. "She had this shoulder-length Titian hair and bright auburn eyes."

"What's her name?" I asked him.

"Brooke. We were only married for a year and three

months."

"What made you break up?" I asked.

He sat silent, staring me down. A shadow crossed his face. "Her death broke us up, Penny."

I couldn't stop the gasp that followed. My hand slapped over my mouth. "Jesus, Oliver, I'm sorry."

He shook his head at me. "It gets worse," he told me, clearing his throat of emotion. I didn't know how that could have been possible, but I waited. "She killed herself."

"Oh my God," I exclaimed.

He sat quietly. I was afraid to speak. A million thoughts ran through my mind.

"Threw herself on the Tube tracks," he explained.

"Oh, Jesus," I whispered. "I'm so sorry, Oliver."

His eyes stared blankly at the plaster ceiling. "I came home one afternoon after visiting my parents. Brooke said she had a few things to get caught up with and had decided not to come with me. I knew it was bullshit, but I thought she might want a few nights to herself and didn't argue with it."

He looked over at me. "She wasn't here when I got back, but I didn't think anything of it. I unpacked, took a shower, then planned to make her dinner. I lit a few candles, put on some music. It was all so normal. It all felt *so normal.*"

I reached for his hand and took it in mine. He squeezed it. "By six o'clock, I started to get worried. All my attempts at trying to ring her hadn't worked. Eventually I started to panic. I rang up all her friends, her parents, and no one had seen her. I was just about to get in my car when my phone buzzed. I remember the feeling of my heart starting to settle down in my chest. I actually felt immediate relief that it was one of her family members or friends calling to tell me she was okay.

"I answered the phone, but it was Scotland Yard. They asked if I was Brooke Finn's husband and I told them I was. They wanted to know if I could come down to the station. I still felt relief that she was there, though I would have preferred she'd just turned her phone off with friends or something, but I was so worked up at that point I was willing to take any explanation. I asked if I needed bail money, but they assured me I didn't.

"Without skipping a beat, I got in the car and drove up to the station. I rushed through the doors, determined to get her out of there as quickly as possible. When I introduced myself to the front desk, they ushered me into an empty room. I thought it was strange but still hadn't put two and two together at that point."

My eyes burned for him. He looked at me, his eyes turning glassy. "I thought she'd just gotten into a bit of trouble is all and they needed to question me or something. I was eager to talk to someone and was growing impatient. Eventually two detectives came in the room. One set a bloody cup of tea in front of me. He asked how I took it. I told them with a little cream. They acted so casually it reassured me more, and my heart settled like a rock in my chest. I felt like I could breathe again.

"That's when they dropped the bomb. I could not believe my ears, Penny. I literally did not believe them. Instant denial. It was instant denial. I kept telling them they'd made a mistake, insisting that Brooke wouldn't do something like that.

"They hit with me undeniable proof in the form of an

envelope with my name printed on the front. They'd already opened it and pored over the contents. I felt ill. I opened the letter and read what she'd written. Immediately, I vomited into the nearest wastebasket.

"I staggered up and forced myself to stand, demanding to see her. They told me I would not be allowed to, that I would *never* see her, and I vomited once more. I racked my brain trying to remember what she'd worn when I left, trying to remember how she'd worn her hair, but couldn't remember. I can't remember what I'd last said to her, Penny. I don't think it was I love you. If it'd been I love you, I'm sure I would've remembered. I still can't remember."

I sucked in a deep breath to steady my voice. "I am so incredibly sorry, Oli."

He nodded his head. "It's been almost three years and the memories are starting to fade."

"That's understandable."

He creased his brows. "Is it, though? I don't think that's normal." He took a deep breath. "I *hate* her."

My eyes clenched and I swallowed. "Why?"

"Drink?" he asked instead of answering.

"Sure, Oli."

He got up and returned with two tumblers and a bottle of Glenlivet. He poured two fingers' worth in each. I sipped at mine. He downed his.

"I can tell you what she'd written in her letter verbatim. I've read it thousands of times. I'll spare you most of it. Here's the good bit, though." He cleared his throat. *"Oliver,* she'd written, *I'm not sure how to tell you this, but there is something that has eaten me from the inside out these last six months and the thought of facing you with the truth of it is too much for me to bear. I've been having an affair with someone. It wasn't planned, but is it ever, really? Not that it is any excuse, but I never intended to hurt you. I want you to know I love you so very dearly, but I've made an irreparable tear in our marriage and it cannot be fixed. Please forgive me. I love you.* She signed it, tucked it into that envelope, and left it taped to a concrete pillar near where she jumped."

He choked back tears. "I don't know why she even bothered to tell me about the affair at that point, you know? What is the point of that? I've fought with myself on that for ages. One minute I'm grateful she admitted to it so I at least knew the reason she'd jumped, sparing me from any personal guilt, but the next minute I loathe her so intensely for telling me. In confessing, she exacerbated the pain exponentially." He watched me with a watery smile. "I know how you feel right now," he told me. "I know that side of infidelity, and I wouldn't wish that on my worst enemy, Penelope. I know that strange mixture of hate and love that's swirling in your heart and head. I am all too familiar with it, and it's everything in me not to run over Graham with my car for it."

I couldn't help it, I smiled through my falling tears. "It's the thought, Oli," I said, reaching up and hugging his neck with my good arm. I choked back tears for him. "I'm so sorry, Oli," I whispered.

He held me at the waist. "We're kindred spirits," he said over my shoulder.

I fell back into my chair with his help. I tossed the rest of my whisky, wincing at the burn as it settled down my throat, and held out my pinky. He wrapped his with mine. "Here's to kindred spirits," he said, breaking our hold, and pouring four more fingers between us.

"To us. To the pain. To it all," I said, raising my glass in the air. His tumbler clinked with mine.

"To it all," he whispered.

We finished the bottle.

Chapter Eight

Oli and I slept until noon, courtesy of the Glenlivet. Oli showed up at my door at 12:03 p.m. with a large glass of water and a pair of aspirin.

"Bless you," my scratchy voice rang through.

He carefully laid beside me on the bed and tucked his arms inside one another. "What the hell were we thinking?" he asked.

I laughed, but it was short lived, killed by the throbbing in my head and an involuntary moan. "We weren't."

"I'm surprised you can hold your own like that, though, Pen. I never saw you drink more than a pint whenever we all went out."

"I don't even remember getting into bed last night. I don't think that's holding my own at all."

He chuckled. "Guess not. Why hadn't I ever seen you drink before, really?" he asked me.

"Look at the evidence, Oli, the one night I did let go, Graham revealed he'd cheated and I fell into a sunken terrace."

"But that's an outlier, not the mean. Why, Penny?"

I forced a smile. "Graham always drank to excess and I couldn't ever let myself get comfortable with him. I needed to stay together in case he needed me."

Oliver looked at me with a worried expression. "Is that truly why, Pen?"

"Yes."

"That's just sad, that. Penny, why would you let anyone control you like that?"

"He didn't *make* me do that. I did that on my own."

He shifted on his side toward me. "Can't you see, though? His knowing he could rely on you so implicitly that way and acting so irresponsibly with drink *was* controlling you."

He was making too much sense, and I had nothing to say to that. He scrutinized my face, and it made me blush under the heat of his gaze.

"How old are you, Pen?" he asked softly.

"Twenty-two" I answered. He bobbed his head up and down. "How old are you?" I asked him.

"I'll be twenty-seven in six weeks."

"That's when I get my leg cast off."

"So it is," he observed with a grin.

"I'll probably be home by then," I told him.

"Why's that?" he asked.

"I've nothing to keep me here once I'm recovered enough to travel, Oliver. I can't stay here where there's no future for me."

"Rubbish."

I giggled at his brashness. "Why do you say that?"

"It's rubbish because you could work from anywhere

in the world at any time, Pen. You are free to live an adventurous life." He fell back and tucked both hands beneath his head. "You should stay here with me until you're fully recovered. We can spend my birthday together. Stay friends with me for a little while here, then decide what you want to do."

I thought over what he said and decided it wasn't an altogether unreasonable suggestion. "What if you get sick of me living with you in two weeks and regret the invitation?"

"Not possible. I've already determined that you're not much of a bother. You're fun to talk to. I don't like living alone like this. Never had, really. And if at the end of our trial run you're still having a good time, we can talk about a roommate-type situation. Then, when you get fed up with us Londoners, you can run off to wherever your heart drags you. It's a perfect situation. You'd be a fool to turn it down."

I laughed softly. "You've made me an offer I cannot refuse," I spouted in my best *Godfather* voice.

"May your first child be a masculine child," Oli added.

"What the hell are you talking about?"

"It's the only *Godfather* line I know.

I laughed loudly at that. "You're a trip, Oli."

We sat in companionable silence for at least an hour and not once did it get uncomfortable, which astonished me.

"Hey," Oli finally said.

"Yeah?"

"I haven't talked about Brooke in over a year, do you know that?"

"Is it hard for you?" I asked.

73

"It is, yes, but I think I only miss what we could have been at this point. I'm not bitter or anything, though. I've forgiven her, don't get me wrong. At first I was too livid to even consider it. The funeral was a roller coaster of emotions for me, but eventually I let my disappointment at what she'd done go and gave it to God. That's when I started praying for her soul. I pray for her every day." He sighed. "It took a while, but I forgave her, though the forgiveness came at a strange time."

"It did?"

"In retaliation for what she'd done, I started sleeping with anything that moved. It was childish, I know, but I was dysfunctional and couldn't wrap my mind around how to care for my broken mind, never mind my broken heart. I should have been in therapy. In fact, I should be in therapy now, but it is what it is. Anyway, for some reason, after the tenth girl, I felt such an inexplicable and incredible guilt. Though Brooke had been dead for six months at that point, it didn't matter. I literally felt like I'd cheated on my wife and, let me tell you, the shame was substantial. I suddenly understood why she hadn't wanted to face me after what she'd done.

"Pen, I wish she had just come to me, told me what happened. Our marriage might not have survived, but at least she'd be alive. She could have started anew, learned to forgive herself, contributed something to this earth other than heartache. I'm not necessarily blaming her for what she did, because I don't know her state of mind then. I like to think she wasn't all there, you know? It helps me to sleep at night, at least."

"What a heavy burden to carry."

"It's okay," he promised. "I might be shedding tiny

pieces of the aftermath still, but nothing like before."

"I think you carry around more than you think still."

"Don't go there, Pen."

I sighed. "Oliver, you still act like a destructive moron."

"Hello, Pot. I'm Kettle."

"How is it I'm the pot?"

"You have been here for eight months, Pen, and I have seen you slowly morph into the girl Graham *wanted* you to be. That's not healthy either."

I bit my tongue. "Change of subject?" I asked.

After a brief moment of silence, he nodded. "What should we do with our weeks?" he asked, agreeing to the truce.

"What can we really do when I'm casted up like this?"

"Lots." He shrugged. "Just have to get creative."

"*Well?* I'm waiting."

"Oh, you need ideas *now*? I don't have anything now. I need time."

"Fine, tonight at dinner. I'll be waiting."

"We could go *out* for dinner tonight, if you want."

"Where to?" I asked.

"The Briargrove?"

"Uh, the Briargrove? You Mr. Moneybags or something?" I glanced around the room. "Oh, wait, I guess you are. Fine then. The Briargrove it is."

"Good."

"Wait, are you paying?"

He laughed. "Yes, of course."

"Since it's such a fancy-shmancy place, I can do myself up real nice-like and turn it into a vlog." I started getting excited. "What do you say? You want to help me?"

"*Me?* Help with your vlog?"

"Yes! You're so *GQ*, the girls will love you. I'll get half-a-million views by the morning and then Clinique will call and shove cash down my pockets to advertise on my super well-liked site with the cute boy!" I blushed when I'd inadvertently complimented him.

"You're mental," he said, batting away my hand when I started to poke him.

"Come on, Oli. Please?"

"What would you have me do anyway?"

"Not sure yet, just agree to it."

"I'll agree but I reserve the right to veto any decision I don't agree with."

I looked at him seriously. "Would you like a safe word?"

He bit his bottom lip in mock worry. "Yes, madam."

"Okay." I thought for a moment. "Your safe word is bumfuzzle."

He laughed then groaned, his hand going to his head. "I am *not* saying that."

"You have to. It's a real word, Oli, I swear. It doesn't mean anything dirty. It's just a great, underused word."

He smiled at me. "What does it mean?"

"It's another word for confuse or perplex and it's brilliant, Oli."

He shook his head, accepting his fate. "How in the bloody hell do you keep talking me into this kind of nonsense?"

I emphatically waved my good hand in excitement then realized something. "Wait, doesn't the Briargrove have a wait list?"

"That they do, Penelope Beckett. That they do, but it

just so happens I might know a fellow who knows a fellow who could get us in."

"You *might* know a guy who knows a guy?"

"Possibly. My old schoolmate is good friends with a guy who may or may not work there, but it is more promising than not."

"It all sounds so credible, we're almost guaranteed a table."

"I know. I'm well connected to people who are well connected."

Chapter
Nine

Oli helped me make my new vlog. I made him wear his three-piece fitted suit when he did it. I could practically hear all the girls around the world sigh. He stood like a butler behind me and would fetch pieces I needed when I playfully snapped my fingers. I had to stop filming a number of times to scold him for laughing. I wore a slip in the video. It wasn't indecent or anything, but it needed to be something I could also put clothes over. The point of the vid was to show how you could look stylish even with monstrosities like casts attached to your legs or arms. I braced Oliver before we began filming but he blushed regardless, which made me blush.

I also filmed myself doing my hair after my shower and decided to make that a small segment in the beginning of the video. The idea of curling my hair was a little daunting so I opted to shake things up a little bit and flat-iron the length, finishing up with a little bit of Bio-Oil to tame the flyaways. It was a chic look. I thought my viewers would enjoy it.

I chose one of my many vintage pieces that Graham made no secret he detested. It was nude in color, a sheer one-piece sheath with an organza pencil skirt that met me at the knees. It was tailored at the waist with an organza-and-lace ruffle that fell a little longer in the back and circled my entire waist. The bodice was a V-neck that fell dramatically in the front and back and was embroidered with tiny clusters of crystals on the lace. Little frog buttons crawled up the back of the bodice to the dip of the V. It was one of my favorite dresses ever.

Oli had a hell of a time putting it on me and when I looked back at the footage, it was beyond comical. My followers would love it. Once it was on, Oli looked a little red in the face from the effort, which made it totally worth it. I'd turned to the camera at that point and said, "No pain, no gain." He'd zipped me up the side and stood to my left like the good pretend butler he was.

When we said goodbye to the cameras and I shut everything down, readying the film for editing later, Oliver fell back on top of the bed.

"How the hell do you do that several times a week? That was a beating!"

I laughed. "Oh, come on, it wasn't that bad."

He sat up, his shoe-clad feet resting on the floor. "Penelope, that was pure torture for me. I had to remind myself it was being filmed to keep my expression in check."

I giggled and hobbled for the wardrobe Oliver had placed all my belongings in for me. I reached for the left shoe of a pair of kitten heels that would go with what I was wearing, but also wouldn't trip me up while I was on the scooter. I sat next to Oli on the bed and handed him the shoe.

"Do you mind? It has an ankle strap."

"Of course, Cinderella," he said, taking the shoe and kneeling on one knee.

He ran his hand down the back of my calf to lift the foot. The warmth of his fingers biting into my skin sent shivers down my spine. *Whoa. Whoa. Whoa. What was that?* I gulped and ignored the reaction his touch gave me.

We both got really quiet and the moment was filled with palpable tension. Realizing this, we each stood up, a little flustered.

Oli cleared his throat. "So, shall we?" he asked, extending an arm.

I forced a smile and disregarded the rush his second touch gave me. "Um, yes," I said a little too brightly.

Oli walked ahead of me and helped me down into the sunken workroom. I fixed my knee on the scooter and pushed forward, awkwardly following him into the kitchen. I didn't know what to do with myself. The dynamic between us had suddenly changed and I didn't want it to, couldn't let it.

Oli swung around. "Can we address what that just was?"

I sighed in relief. "Let's."

"That was a bit odd, right?"

"It really was." I laughed.

"What are we supposed to do now?" he asked, looking a little green around the collar.

"Oli, calm down! You're a boy. I'm a girl. We've spent a lot of time together nonstop these last few days, we've admitted stuff to each other. It's a growing friendship. Sometimes people confuse these feelings with attraction."

He looked disappointed, but I couldn't be sure. "Yes, of course. Um, yes, you're right." He took a deep breath and released it. "You're right."

"See? No big deal! We just need to establish a few boundaries."

"Boundaries, yes. Establish boundaries," he repeated like a parrot.

"We'll just play it cool with each other. I'm still pissed right now about Graham, and approaching even more confusing feelings, I can feel it, and we can't complicate matters. Plus, well, you're still dealing with the remnants of Brooke."

"Not really," he denied.

"Kettle, please stop."

"Fine."

"Let's go to dinner and forget all about it," he said, running a hand down his mouth.

"Sounds like a plan," I said.

He tugged the linked cuffs of his crisp shirt out of the arms of his jacket and pulled at his collar and the bottom of his vest. "Let's go," he said, making a beeline toward the workroom.

Oli helped me into the car then got in himself and started the engine. "Shit," he said.

"What?"

"I forgot to call Ronnie, see if he got in touch with his mate at the Briargrove."

"Call him now, I guess?"

He picked up his phone, dialed his friend, and I waited.

"Ronnie, it's Oliver." Pause. "Yeah, mate. Yeah, course, course." Oli laughed that unnatural laugh all boys laugh when they're talking with their friends. I rolled my eyes at him. He shrugged his shoulders in question, but I waved him on. "Yeah, that sounds good, mate. Let's do that then. Give me a ring next week sometime, will ya?" Pause. "Not at all, mate. No worries." Another fake laugh. "Right, then. Right. Talk to you then."

He hung up.

"No table," he said in his normal tone.

I wasn't that disappointed. The Briargrove was swanky and the food was excellent, but there wasn't such a thing as relaxing in places like that. It was not a casual experience by any means.

"Oh well," I told him. "How about another place?"

"I should have made backup reservations at other places. Now nothing will be available," he told me.

"Who cares? We'll go someplace that doesn't require a reservation."

Oliver and I had a roaring good time at some hilarious, kitschy little dinner theater. We spent the next several days running errands together, cooking together, working together, though he didn't costar with me in another vlog again, which was disappointing because the one with him had gone viral with more than two million views in less than four days. Generally we were becoming better friends, but we never crossed any line with one another. We created boundaries and kept within them, which was good for us. I'd never had a male friend who was genuine like Oliver. We had fun together while I healed, and each day it got easier and easier to move around as I got accustomed to my casts. He took me to get my secondary X-rays the following Friday morning and I got the thumbs up that everything was healing quite nicely.

There wasn't really anything we avoided talking about, besides the random spark we'd felt the morning of our shared vlog. Well, that and the fact we both knew he was going to be seeing Graham that night.

When we got home from the doctor's office around three in the afternoon or so, I told him I was going to do another vlog and to shout at me on his way out.

I rolled toward my room, but he jogged beside me on the way there. "You're not going to do the girl thing, right, and get pissed I'm leaving to hang out with your ex, are you?"

I stopped rolling and he stood beside me. "You want what you want to hear, or do you want the truth?" I asked him.

"Damn it, Penny," he said, walking toward his chair and sinking into it.

I sat on the cushion of my scooter. My good hand went to my face and dragged down. "Hear me out, Oli."

"Fine," he huffed, "let's hear it then."

"I'm not an idiot. I know you've been friends since you were small, so I'm not gonna do the chick thing and start making demands, 'cause that doesn't work and I don't really want to even tell you what to do. I hate being ordered around and spouting them leaves a bad taste in my mouth. I'm just gonna say this one thing: *please don't trust him*. Ever. Keep your friendship at shallow level so you'll be protected."

"You can't say that, Penny. It's past the point of no return. It'd be unnatural to lower it to superficial after twenty years."

"You're right," I conceded with a sigh. "Can you just

not talk about me with him then?"

He nodded and offered a sweet smile. "That I can definitely do."

Two hours later, when I was in the middle of edits, Oliver knocked on my door and I called out for him to come in.

"Looking sharp, kid!" I told him, spinning around in my chair.

He ran the palms of his hands over his glossed hair. Oliver had one of those haircuts that could be whatever you wanted it to be. He could style it to look like he was Jimmy Darmody one minute then the next day would let it dry naturally and pull the front forward messily. It was constantly evolving. I kind of dug it but didn't want to admit that to myself. I shook my head to clear it.

"I'm just to the pub then," he said. "I'll lock up and set the perimeter alarms. Call if you need to leave for whatever reason and I'll walk you through it." I smelled his cologne as he bent over the desk near me. I held my breath so I wouldn't have to scent him. He wrote down six numbers on a scrap sheet of paper with my pencil. "That's the code, just in case. Call if you need anything," he said, kissing my cheek and jetting off.

I let out the dizzying breath I'd held and my fingers went to the skin he'd kissed. *Ignore it. Ignore it. Ignore it,* I chanted.

"Catch you later!" I yelled in an attempt to sound normal, but didn't really succeed.

I went back to my editing and after a few minutes found myself in a distracted groove, which helped all the warring emotions fighting inside.

When the windows had grown dark and I'd grown

sufficiently hungry, I orchestrated the dip from my room into the workroom then rolled into the kitchen to help myself to something to eat. On Oliver's fridge was a taped note.

I made you a little plate so you wouldn't have to go rummaging on that bum leg of yours. - Oliver

Inside the fridge was a plate of grapes, crackers, cheese, and prosciutto. Beside that was a chilled bottle of white with a note that read: *Drink me, Penny.* There was a corkscrew on the counter and I popped that baby open, pouring some into a tea mug because I'm classy like that. I scarfed down the food and played sudoku on my phone while I did.

When I'd put everything up, I retreated to my room. Just as I sat, I got a text. Bringing the phone to my face, I could see the text was from Graham but could only read the first portion of his message. My stomach plummeted as I slid to unlock my phone.

Expected you to be here with oliver. U looked pretty chummy together the other day. Are you sleeping with him?

I didn't want to respond. I knew I shouldn't have responded. But I did.

Don't text me anymore

I bet you are, he responded.

My blood coursed through my body at a furious pace.

Stop

I bet you are I wouldn't put it past you to do something like that

I pressed the top button of my phone with shaky fingers to close out the screen altogether and set it at the top corner of my desk, as out of sight as possible. Every time the phone vibrated, I jumped. Each time felt like a knife to the heart, reminding me of what he'd done. They came to me for fifteen minutes straight. I couldn't take it anymore and I grabbed the phone, reading each one in turn.

Has it not occurred to you that he's MY best mate? It's wrong you're staying with him

What kind of girl runs to her ex's friend for comfort? Did you fall on purpose?

Chloe thinks you did and I'm wondering now if that's exactly what you did

Why would you be staying with Oliver otherwise

Does Oliver know how much you hated him before I broke up with you

I wonder if I told him what he would do

Answer me or I'll tell him

The last one had popped up while I was reading. My fingers couldn't type fast enough.

I'm not yours to control anymore, I told him. Go back to your French Jezebel. Leave me alone.

Graham didn't respond; I felt my stomach settle once again. I breathed a sigh of relief and went back to my edits. Five minutes later my phone rang. I looked down for the ID and saw it was actually Oli.

"Penelope Beckett, wanton goddess and all-around badass," I answered.

"Penny!" Oliver shouted into the phone. He started to speak, but I couldn't hear him. It was too loud.

"I can't hear you, Oli!" I shouted back.

"Hold on," he said. It got quiet. "Outside now. Are you texting Graham?" he asked.

"Just to tell him to leave me alone."

"Oh my God, Pen. Stop. No matter what he says, don't respond."

"Oliver, he's saying some vile things! I had to."

I could hear him sigh. "I know him and he is trying to keep open the line of communication for no other reason than he just likes the control, so don't give in."

"Fine. I won't. I'll just sit here in my little chair and mind my own business and do my edits."

"Good girl."

"Bye, Ols. Go have fun."

"Bye, Penny."

I finished my vlog and uploaded it to my scheduler then sat down on the bed to watch a little television. Before I knew it, I'd fallen asleep.

Chapter
Ten

I heard a sharp bang as the metal door in Oliver's workroom burst open and I launched up, my breaths panting with the panic. I glanced at the digital clock on the television. It shone 2:37 in the morning. My heart raced in my chest, I stood and felt around for a crutch, determined to use it as a weapon if I had to, but heard Oliver's voice slur something and a girl laughing. I placed the crutch back against the wall and sat at the edge of the bed, cringing at the thought that Oli had brought a girl home with him. I heard another guy's voice, but it wasn't Oli's. No, no, it wasn't Oliver's. It was a voice I knew very well. It was Graham's. I felt ill.

Please just let him be dropping off a drunk Oli. Please. Please. Please.

"Penelope!" Graham's voice rang through the door of my room.

My mouth draped open in shock. I stood, more pissed than I had ever been at him since the whole thing had gone down, and hobbled toward the door, throwing it open. Inside Oli's workroom stood at least fifteen people, and there were more piling through. They all stood quiet and staring at me. I glanced down at my clothes, realizing I was in an old pair of volleyball shorts because they were comfortable to sleep in as well as flexible enough to fit around my leg cast and a tank top because I hadn't any intention of being seen in either. I grabbed my short kimono robe hanging behind the door and draped it over myself, cinching the belt at the waist as best I could.

"Uh, hey," I told the silent room.

"Did we wake you, Pen?" Oliver's raspy voice asked.

"That's okay," I told him, throwing my hair behind my shoulder.

"Why don't you join us, darling?" a lilting French accent asked me.

"No," I bit out just as Oli shouted *yes* with slurred speech.

He was three sheets to the wind.

"Come on, Pen." Oliver waved a sloppy hand my direction. His face held a large, goofy grin.

Graham watched me with rapt attention, his eyes burrowing through me. Just looking at him was painful. I didn't want to be anywhere near him, but I also didn't want him to see me run away. He'd know it was him, and I was tired of him feeling as if he had power over me.

I hopped down the steps and rested my knee on my scooter. Oliver came over and threw a heavy arm around my shoulders. "You know the lads, of course," he mumbled, "but this here," he said, pointing at a blonde I didn't know, "is Gemma." He pointed at another girl, a redhead. "I'm sorry, love, what was your name again?"

"'Allo," the redhead called out in a cockney accent,

"I'm Nicki."

He pointed out three more girls I wouldn't remember the names of and thankfully skipped over Chloe, buried in Graham's embrace and smiling at me as if she'd won some grand prize, which she most definitely had not.

"Music then?" he asked the group, and everyone followed him into the kitchen where he plugged his phone into a Bose speaker. Tunes covered the silence, giving me a bit of a reprieve from the strange stares I was getting from everyone.

I felt so uncomfortable; I could practically read their thoughts through their capricious looks. I felt like a fool, a Yank on the wrong side of the pond, and I wasn't wanted. They were loyal to a fault to Graham, and I was someone he wanted gone, so they did as well, save for Oliver. My breaths came in pants as the room seemed to close in on me. I backed up, leaving the scooter where it sat, and rested a hand against the nearest wall for support, heading toward my bedroom. I was escaping and hoped no one noticed.

"Where are you going, Penelope?" Graham asked.

I dared not turn around. "Very tired," I answered with my head toward the ground. "Good night, all."

"Oh come now," Graham prodded. I heard footsteps approach and panicked at the thought he might touch me.

He drunkenly clasped me around the waist and dragged me back toward the group, setting me down in the center of their round configuration. I turned around and searched the crowd for Oliver, but he was gone. So was Gemma.

"Excuse me," I said, trying to break past Graham.

Chloe watched me with hateful eyes.

"Stay, Penelope," Graham insisted. "Join us."

Individual conversations came to a stop as they waited for me to make a decision. I felt trapped. I gulped and sank into a kitchen chair buried on the other side of the group opposite Graham and Chloe. The hurt their presence brought me was growing exponentially. I gripped the edge of my chair to keep from toppling over. *I've made a huge mistake*, I thought, my eyes burning and growing blurry.

"And back to the kitchen!" a cheerfully buzzed Oli sang out. He was playing tour guide to Gemma. Just seeing him made my heart calm and the tears cease. *Friend, albeit stupid, drunk friend,* my thoughts registered. I took a deep breath.

Oli came through and plopped next to me. "Penny, I thought you were in bed," he told me. A hand went to his head, messing up his hair. He didn't bother to fix it. "Oh no! Did we wake you?"

He was so drunk he was confused. "It's all right," I told him, trying to ignore the presence of Graham and the excruciating pain he was causing me. "Did you have fun?" I asked him.

My hand went to my chest, the site of the misery, and rubbed.

"I had a bloody good time, Pen. Lots to drink." He laughed and gestured with his hands down his tall, lean body.

"I can see that," I stated, my hand still rubbing at the hurt.

His eyes went to my fingers and he stilled. "Why are you doing that?" he slurred.

I let my hand drop. "Doing what?"

His eyes widened. "Did I cause that?" he asked, panicked. He pointed at my chest.

"No," I whispered. We were getting stares. Graham's pierced me in my place. It was too heavy to ignore.

I whipped my head his way and narrowed my eyes, a silent threat to leave me alone. I turned back toward Oliver.

"I did that, didn't I?" he asked. He reached out, pressing the butt of his right palm into the agonizing spot. His left hand gripped my shoulder to bring me closer to him. "I forgot," he whispered. "I remembered too much of myself and only myself and forgot you here." He glanced over at Graham, as if just remembering him. "I let him in here. I'm so fucking sorry, Pen."

Shocking everyone around us, including me, Oli stood in a rush, almost toppling over. The movement pushed his chair back, causing it to tip over with a loud clang.

"Everyone out," he gritted, staring down at me.

Oliver's friends, old and new, looked at him with strange expressions. Only his old friends recognized he was serious and started gathering and walking toward his workroom.

I looked over at Graham. He stayed where he stood, his hands clenched. Chloe clambered at his arm in desperation, obviously recognizing something in him she wanted to get control of. It hurt she knew him well enough to see that in him.

"Are you sleeping with her?" Graham shouted. He threw himself forward and stepped to Oliver, nose to nose. They stood at the same height, their chests heaving. Chloe screamed and clawed at Graham's jacket. Oliver's fists clenched, ready to punch, and everyone stopped, trying, in their inebriated states, to gauge whether they should intervene or just watch.

Using the back of my chair for support, my hand still clenched at my chest, I dragged myself up, almost hyperventilating. I let go of the throbbing pain and as calmly as I could, placed a hand on Oliver's chest and pushed gently. The gesture broke his stare on Graham and he staggered back. His eyes looked clearer, though. The burning adrenaline had sobered him. The room was so silent you could hear a pin drop.

I turned to Graham just as he took advantage of Oliver's distraction, bent his arm back and swung, hitting Oliver in the left eye.

I screamed as Oliver staggered back a few steps then regained his footing, a look of pure hate across his face. He cocked his arm back and began to charge.

"No!" I said, putting myself between them, that same hand going to Oliver's chest.

He stopped and looked down on me, his face softening. I turned back toward Graham.

"You're an asshole," I told him matter-of-factly. "And not that it matters, but we are not sleeping together. Oliver took pity on me and gave me a place to stay while I recovered from my *accidental* fall," I rationalized. "I think with all the alcohol you've obviously drunk tonight that anything *other* than your leaving right now would be a very bad idea. Leave."

Graham looked at me, then at my hand still resting on Oliver's chest. A strange look I recognized as regret fell upon his face. I knew Graham, though, and any regret he felt could only be selfish. Eventually Graham's stance relaxed and he walked backward a few steps before turning around and grabbing Chloe on his way out. I removed my hand from Oliver's chest and brought it to my own, to that painful spot, and pressed. The rest of the group fell behind Graham and when the door closed, I relaxed. I turned to Oli and tried to put on a good-humored face, but the expression on his confused me.

He looked down at my chest where I had plastered my good hand. "I did that. I put that there," he said. His brows pinched in pain, in obvious disappointment in himself. His left eye was starting to swell.

I reached up and dragged my thumb over his forehead. "Stop it, Oli," I told him softly. "You know damn well you didn't put that pain there."

"I may not have put it there, but I made it throb where otherwise it would and should have subsided. I clawed at the wound."

"Oli—" I began, but he stopped me by wrapping me in a hug.

"I'm sorry. Very sorry," he said. He brought his lips to my ear. My hair shifted with each breath he took. "I'm drunk, Pen," he whispered.

I laughed. "I know, Oli. Come on," I said, breaking away. His warm skin overwhelmed me and I struggled between the butterflies it gave me and the broken heart that barely beat in my chest. "Let's get you to bed."

He nodded and after I grabbed a plastic bag, filled it with ice, and yanked a hand towel from its drawer, I hobbled/led him back toward his bedroom, a room I had yet to see for myself.

We rounded the hall off the kitchen and landed in a room at the back that, frankly, wasn't anything at all like I'd expected. It was a dark room, though I did expect that, but it was much richer and warmer than I imagined. For some reason, I expected something modern, but it was nothing like that. There were two exposed brick walls and a large hide patchwork carpet over the original wood floor. I wondered briefly if he'd made it and decided to remember to ask him about it later.

The bed was four poster and painted metal but cast to look like bamboo. The headboard was an intricate lattice pattern with Asian-inspired elements draped throughout the canopy frame. There was a huge block of rattan caning at the headboard and footboard. The bedding itself was simple white linen and down. It looked utterly masculine yet not overly so. Oli wasn't overcompensating like Graham did. I was only just realizing how different Graham and Oliver were.

He fell face-first onto the bed and groaned as he attempted to pull off his vest, his face still buried in his comforter.

"My eye," he moaned.

I sat at the edge of the bed beside him. "Where's your jacket, Oliver?"

"In the car. I treated it very badly. It'll have to be dry-cleaned."

"Don't worry about that now."

"I won't," he said. He turned his head in that languid manner that drunks adopted. "Are you upset with me?" he asked, sounding worried.

"I'm not," I told him, handing him the makeshift ice pack.

"I can't believe I did this," he said, taking it. "*You* may not be mad, but I'm angry at myself. And I'm sorry."

"It's okay, Oliver." I swallowed. "But this night did tell

me something."

"What's that?" he asked.

"I think I need to get out of London. Just for a little while. I need distance. I feel like the wound scabs only to be reopened over and over."

He nodded. "I have an idea then, Penelope."

"What's that?" I asked.

"I'll finish up my last order tomorrow and we'll go on a trip, you and I."

"Together? Where to? I can't fly, remember?"

"It's not far. I'll take you to my childhood home. You can meet my family. They're a good sort, and I like them very much. They bring me comfort. I suspect my mother will bring you that as well. She's a sweet woman."

I smiled at him. "Will I meet your sister, the handbag designer?"

He laughed. "Yes, you will. And all her little monsters as well. How are you with children?"

"Oh, I'm the queen of children. They love me. I think it's because I hand out candy like water and can spend hours chasing them around." I stared down at my leg cast. "Not that I'll be able to do that with them, which is a shame. I'll have to double up on candy."

Oliver, though he laid like a lump, laughed, shaking the bed. "My sister's husband will love that, I suspect," he said sarcastically.

"He's none of my concern. Children are more my speed."

"That's sort of lovely, Penny."

I looked at him, wondering if he really meant it. "Well, I am what I am and that's all that I am."

"Good on you, Popeye."

"What's your sister's name?" I asked him.

Oliver lazily turned over on his back, forgetting all about his vest.

I leaned over him and slowly undid the buttons for him. His hooded eyes watched me. I averted my gaze so my hands wouldn't shake any more than they already were. When I reached the bottom, I laid the flaps back. He shrugged it off and I took it from him, folded it neatly, and placed it on his nightstand. When I sat back down, he grabbed my wrist, and my heart leapt into my throat.

"Thank you," he told me.

"You're welcome," I said and sat back.

He let go of my wrist and stared at the ceiling.

"Oli?"

"Yes?"

"Your sister's name?"

He cleared his throat. "My sister's name is Zoe. She's ten years older and talks to me like I'm one of her children," he explained, but he was smiling so I could tell he didn't mind. "My mother is Eleanor and my dad is George."

"Eleanor, George, and Zoe. Got it."

He smiled at me. "What are you parents' names?"

"Ben and Samantha."

"Do you have any siblings?"

"Two brothers, Sam and Mark."

"Older or younger?"

"Both older."

"You're the baby of the family then? How did they feel about your moving to jolly old England?"

I laughed. "They really, *really* thought it was a terrible idea. For weeks while I waited for my resident visa they tried everything to convince me to stay. I'd just graduated university and was offered a pretty nice job in Dallas. I'd already had the vlog and had begun to make a little bit of income and I thought since I was young," I said, hesitating on the next bit, "and i-in love, I could have a little adventure and just see where it took me."

"That's understandable." He cleared his throat. "Do you regret coming here?"

"I don't believe in regrets, not really. I mean, in the heat of a moment I may strongly wish I hadn't done something, but to be honest, I believe all our decisions help mold us into the persons we're supposed to become. Think about it, if everyone made flawless decisions, how could any of us truly understand life and all its accompanying beauties? If we never suffer, how can we recognize joy for what it is? If we never witness another's struggles, how can we submit ourselves to helping them? No regrets help shape us into selfless people. After all, the only regrets people really speak of are surrounded by a hesitation to love or allow love."

"Jesus, Penelope." Oliver's brows furrowed as his eyes pored me over. "I think Graham is a genuine fool."

I ran my good hand over the top of his soft comforter. "We're all fools, but between Graham and myself, I was the bigger one."

"There you are wrong. You're not a fool, Pen. You may have lost yourself a little bit when you got with him, but you'll get it back."

"I'm feeling insecure right now, so I'm just going to take your word for it."

"There's a quote from Ernest Hemingway's *Men Without Women* that goes 'The most painful thing is losing yourself in the process of loving someone too much, and forgetting that you are special too.'"

"That's beautiful."

"Agreed," he said, throwing an arm over his head.

"It is unbelievably unfair that you can be poetic even in your inebriated state," I teased.

His head lolled toward me and he gave me a devastating smile. It did something to my stomach, that smile. I needed an escape. I began to stand to leave, but he grabbed my good arm. "Do you need help?" he asked me as if he could be useful.

"No, thank you."

"Good night, Popeye."

"Night, Ernest."

Chapter
Eleven

The next day, I sat with Oliver as he finished his work and got it ready for shipment. He placed it in a gorgeous blue velvet cloth case and several layered boxes. The last box he bound with linen twine and set that inside a shipping container full of plastic air pockets. It was all so beautifully done. I was so incredibly impressed with his whole setup. He left me at home to ship it somewhere up north and while he was gone, I got an idea.

It was a risk, but I decided it was worth it. With as much care as possible, I set the handbag Oliver made with his sister Zoe on his gorgeous bed, because the light was perfect in the room, and filmed it in several sequences, capturing all sides, making sure to get all details, and then returned the bag to its cabinet.

I edited the film and recorded a voiceover highlighting the details of the bag as well as the quality and even spoke about a brief history of his family. I did it in less than an hour then edited it all together. I watched the whole thing and was rather proud of it.

When Oli got home I called him into the room and showed it to him.

"Right. That's insane, Pen. Did you do all this whilst I was away?" he asked, incredulous.

"I did! Do you like it?"

He nodded. "But what was it for?"

"I think you should market those bags, Oli. I think they would sell better than you could possibly imagine."

"I don't know, Pen," he said, rubbing the back of his neck.

"Oh no, I've made you uncomfortable. If you don't want to do it, it's not a big deal! This video I made on a whim."

"No, that's not it at all. Actually, I think it'd be nice to branch off and do something kind of different. Expand my horizons and all that."

"I sense a but in there."

"I'm just not sure Dad would want me to is all."

"Oh, then never mind. No big deal." I smiled.

"Let's show Mum and Zoe, though, they'll love it."

"Okay, I'll privately upload it on my server and when you remember, we can get to it."

"Are you all packed?" he asked me, pointing toward my canvas suitcase.

I stood, balanced on my good foot and saluted him. "Aye, aye, Captain!"

"All aboard then," he said and grabbed my bag, then looked at it. He smiled at me.

"Be right back," he said, tossing my canvas bag back down on the bed.

He came back in with *the* bag and handed it to me.

I giggled. "What?"

"It's yours. Take it."

"No!" I exclaimed. "No way!"

"Why the hell not?" he asked, looking genuinely hurt.

"I couldn't. It wouldn't feel right."

"Bollocks! It's just a bit of leather. I can make another, and you obviously love it." I shook my head but he pushed the bag at me. "It's just been sitting in the cabinet for a year doing nothing. Just take it, Pen."

I bit my bottom lip and pondered the gift. "What would you charge for this bag if it you were selling it?" I asked.

"What does it matter?" he asked.

"Just tell me. What would you charge for this?"

He wrapped his long hands around the backs of his triceps and shrugged. "I don't know, maybe six thousand pounds?"

My chin dropped to my chest. "Six *thousand* pounds?"

"It does seem sort of ridiculous when you hear it out loud, but that's what I would charge for it. When you put together the history, the grueling training, the tools, and the time, that's what Finn leather is worth."

"That is," I told him, examining the bag, taking in the craftsmanship, then meeting his eyes, "understandable."

He ducked his head and his cheeks turned pink. "Well, thank you, Miss Beckett."

I handed the bag over to him. "As generous as it was to offer it to me, I couldn't possibly take something with that much value."

"You're being a brat, Pen."

I laughed. "Stop, Oli, it's just too much. It'd make me uncomfortable."

He sighed. "Right, well, I can't allow you to feel

uncomfortable. I'm English after all. It'd be a betrayal," he teased.

He set the bag on my bed, grabbed my canvas one, and helped me into the car, loading everything in, including my oh-so-sexy scooter. Oli escaped back inside and locked everything up.

"Road tunes," he ordered when he'd climbed into the driver's side.

I held up my phone. "I made a playlist just for this occasion. Get ready to rock," I told him, grabbing his jack cord and plugging it into my phone.

Blondie's "The Tide is High" played and Oliver laughed.

"Sit tight," I told him, bouncing my shoulders and shimmying in my seat, "it's going to be an eclectic ride."

"You're kind of a trip, Popeye."

Winking at his compliment, I broke into song and took my hair out of its ponytail, shaking out the curls. I stuck a dashcam on his dashboard.

"Just go with it!" I yelled over the music.

He shrugged his shoulders. I checked my makeup in the mirror and flipped it back up then bent forward to turn on the camera. I hoped to use a sped-up version of the footage as part of a montage for the beginning of my next vlog since the girls loved Oli, not that it was surprising, and were requesting more of him. I was happy to oblige.

He turned down the music and asked, "Right. I have to stop for petrol, use the toilet, get sorted. Need anything?"

"That was quite possibly the most English thing you've ever said. You're only missing 'bugger' and 'bloody.' And no, thank you."

He stepped out of the car and turned around. "Don't roll down your window for any of these bloody buggers," he teased.

"There you go."

He smiled. "I'm serious, though."

I saluted him again. "Yes, sir."

He closed the door and filled the tank, then stepped inside the gas station.

We hit the M4 in record time and arrived in Bray Village in about forty-five minutes. We pulled onto his parents' gravel drive as butterflies attacked my stomach. I took deep, even breaths to control them. *I don't need this. Please, go away*, I begged them. Oli rolled down his window and pressed a button on the receiver box outside a pair of swooping wood gates.

"Bankside," a posh woman's accent greeted, "can I help you?"

"Mum, it's me. I'm a bit early."

"Oliver!" she shouted. "Come quick, George, Oliver's here."

We heard shuffling through the small speaker. "How's it?" a man's voice asked.

"Dad, open the gate!" Oli shouted into the receiver.

He sat back in the car and looked over at me, happily shaking his head in bogus impatience. The butterflies ensued at an exponential rate. *What is wrong with me?* I turned off the dashcam and stuck it into my camera bag.

The automatic gate shifted open slowly and our tires popped and cracked against the gravel drive. The house was a cream brick with gables peppered over several terra cotta sweeping rooflines. He pulled around to the left and parked his car facing the river. I waited for Oli to open my door, which was something Graham had never done for me. With every kindness Oliver offered me, the love I thought I felt for Graham fell through to the earth in small bits of burning ash. Oliver was a soothing reminder of what Graham should have been. I was beginning to hope things I wasn't supposed to hope for with Oliver, which was confusing as hell.

"Ready?" he asked, reaching for me and helping me out of the car.

"As ready as I'll ever be."

"What's wrong, Beckett?"

"I'm not sure?" It came out more as a question than a statement.

"You okay?"

"I just want to make a good impression," I told him.

"No worries, Popeye. They'll love you."

My scooter wouldn't roll over the gravel, so Oli tucked an arm behind my back and swooped me up beneath the knees. I whooped at the movement and felt my cheeks burn when I spotted three faces in the windows of a pair of French doors facing the gravel drive. My hand went to the seat of my heart-print flowy pleated shorts.

Instead of putting me down in front of the doors like I thought he would, Oli signaled with a nod of his head for his parents to open the doors for me, so he crossed the threshold with me in his arms. I was both thrilled and mortified at the act.

I squirmed down from his arms and he laughed at me, helping me stand, even boldly straightening out my shorts in the back.

He stood. "Mum, Dad, Zoe," he greeted. "This is

Penelope Beckett, a Yank with a terrible mouth who hates English cooking."

I felt my face flame. "Oli!" I scolded. I turned toward his family. "Those are atrocious lies. I do not have a terrible mouth and, truthfully, though I'm not necessarily a massive fan of English cooking, I would never say that I hated it."

"How's that for a qualifier?" Oli prodded.

I refrained from socking him in the mouth, but just barely.

His family snorted and laughed, used to his shenanigans apparently.

"Oliver Finn, you've made this poor girl uneasy, you cheeky git," his mother scolded. She kissed his cheek and faced me.

I stuck out my hand for his mom and introduced myself. "Eleanor, it's a pleasure to meet you."

She shook it and smiled so large I genuinely worried it would stick that way. "Mutual, darling."

When she let go, I reached for Oliver's dad's hand and he shook it as well. "George," he introduced himself. "Welcome to our home."

"Thank you. It's so nice to meet you."

I turned toward Zoe. "Hello, love," she greeted.

Eleanor invited us all to sit at her kitchen table for a cup of tea, so Oli helped me to the table and we all sat.

"Oliver told us what happened, dearie," Eleanor said, gently patting the top of my arm cast after setting my cup in front of me.

She pushed a creamer pitcher and a bowl of sugar cubes my direction and I took it from her, helping myself to two lumps and a bit of milk.

"I told them about your fall down that sunken terrace," he said, not mentioning Graham directly. He let that be my call, which I appreciated. My stomach filled with butterflies again as he looked at me. *Oh my God! You have to stop this!*

"Yes, it was a terrible night," I explained to his family. "Penny takes a tumble and all that. I was a little distracted that night."

"You look to be on the mend, though," Zoe said kindly.

"I know," Eleanor said. "How'd you get your hair this way, love?" she said as she reached out to finger a curled wave.

"Takes practice, and now that I have the cast, lots of time." I laughed. "I enjoy it, so that helps."

"You're beautiful, Penelope," Eleanor complimented. "What say you, George?" Eleanor asked her husband.

He smiled sweetly. "You're just lovely, dearie," he concurred.

This is the way of the English. Very complimentary, almost overly so, but oh-so genuine and kind. The eight months I'd gotten to spend there before Graham had left me introduced me to a style of speaking that I had never experienced. I'd grown to really love and respect the English because of it. They were such a wonderful people.

A tall, balding man came into the kitchen towing three children with him. One of those a baby no older than six months or so. I itched to hold her. They were a loud, overdone theatrical performance when they came through. The two older children, a boy and a girl, squealed and ran to their grandparents then realized Oliver was there and ran over to him in shouts and giggles, pulling on his sleeves and kissing on his cheeks.

It took a moment for them to realize a stranger sat amongst them.

"Right. Who's this then?" the man asked. He turned to Oliver. "Oli, you've brought a girl home with you?" he asked. He sounded perplexed.

Oliver laughed.

Eleanor leaned toward me. "Oliver's not brought a girl home since," she hesitated, "well, in several years."

I knew who she meant but kept my mouth shut. "I'm a novelty, eh?" I asked, elbowing Oli playfully.

"In more ways than the one," he teased.

"I am *unique*," I acknowledged, hoping they caught the self-deprecation in my tone.

Oli winked at me and I breathed a sigh of relief. For some reason it felt really important that his family liked me.

Oli remembered himself. "Arthur, this is Penelope Beckett. Penny, this is Arthur, Zoe's husband."

Arthur had a jolly face with exaggerated features. His smile was something for the record books and even though he was balding, he was still a handsome man.

"A pleasure." Arthur introduced himself by offering a hand, which I took.

"Arthur, likewise."

Arthur sat down next to his wife and gave her a big kiss on her cheek. Zoe laughed.

"How do you two know one another?" Arthur asked me.

All the blood drained from Zoe's and Eleanor's faces. I'd wondered if they knew, and their expressions were confirmation of it. I took a deep breath.

"Oh, I dated Oli's best friend and we recently broke

up. Oliver's been a good friend to me through it all," I explained away. It was more an attempt at making sure none of his family felt awkward than to diminish what was going on. What was the use of dredging up all the horrifying details? It would do none of us any good.

"Oh, that's terrible for you," Arthur offered kindly.

"It's okay," I told him through a watery smile. "Rather, it will be okay," I told him, trying to keep myself together.

Recognizing the emotion in my voice, Arthur changed the subject.

"Come for a visit, have you?" he asked Oli.

"Yes, wanted to see the rug rats," he said, kissing the top of his baby niece's head.

"They are gorgeous," I told Zoe, which made her beam.

"This is Imogen," Oli said, bouncing the baby in his arms, which earned him a happy squeal. "This is Archie and Sophia."

"Hello, darlins!" I told them. "Come here," I ordered.

Sophia bounced in front of me and Archie followed behind. I reached for my bag but realized I'd left it in the car.

"Oh, Oliver! I've left my bag. Can you get it for me?"

"Your wish is my command," he said, handing the baby over to her mother.

"I've brought presents," I told them. "I never go anywhere where children are without any."

Sophia clapped. "I love pressies!" she told me.

Archie was appropriately excited for any pre-pubescent boy, which is to say he was dying inside but couldn't actually show it or he'd betray himself as not being the man he wanted everyone to think he was.

Soon Oliver emerged with my bag and I dug out my gifts. I turned to Zoe. "Oli promised me they were allowed candy," I told her. She laughed and nodded. I turned back to the kids and handed both of them a bag full of funny and sweet candy.

Sophia jumped up and down, and I teared up at the pleasure it gave her. Archie's face bloomed a little.

"Thank you," he told me.

"You're welcome, sugar."

"Yes! Thank you, thank you, thank you!" Sophia exclaimed.

"That was very sweet of you," Zoe told me. She smiled at her children.

"I have a few nephews and nieces back home. I am quite up to speed on what makes them happy." I sat back in my chair. "Is there anything better than watching happy children?"

"No, indeed," Oliver chimed in, enjoying his nieces and nephews. "There is not."

"May I?" I asked Zoe, gesturing to Imogen.

"Of course not, dearie. Go on then," she said, handing over the baby.

Oliver helped me situate Imogen on my lap where I could hold her comfortably and smell the top of her beautiful baby head.

"The fountain of youth," I told the table. I kissed Imogen's neck and she giggled, making me so happy inside.

I kept Imogen on my lap and we all chatted for half an hour before Eleanor and George got up to start dinner preparations. Zoe and Arthur stood to ration out the candy I'd brought and to clean up any messes their children might have caused, which left myself, Oli, and Imogen at the table on our own.

"Feeling better?" he asked.

I looked at Oliver. "I believe this was just the trick," I told him, cooing at the baby in my arms.

He smiled that sort of smile that screamed contentment. It was the most mellow I'd ever seen Oliver.

"You're very good with children," he told me.

I smelled Imogen's head once more. "I told you I was."

"It's one thing to hear it and quite another to see it."

I looked up at him. "Have you ever thought of having children?" I asked him.

"Loads of times."

"And what was the verdict?" I asked.

"I'd love a few of them running 'round, yeah. They're great."

"Agreed," I told him. "Here," I said, gesturing for Oliver to take Imogen. "I've got to pee like a racehorse."

"The loo's just around that corner," he told me, pointing through the kitchen into a den area and beyond to a short hall.

I rode my scooter with confidence since there was no other way to make the thing look cool. I rounded the bend down the hall and found the door to the restroom where I did my business and washed my hands. When I came back out, Sophia was waiting for me.

"I've been told to come fetch you for dinner," she said with a gigantic purple smile.

"Was the candy good?" I asked her.

"It's been lovely!" she told me, clasping her hands.

I giggled at how wonderful I thought she was. "How old are you, Sophia?"

"Ten."

"Oh, that's a great age," I told her as I rolled back toward the kitchen.

"I think it's just terrible!" she whined. "I can't do anything I want to do. My parents think I'm a baby."

"Oh, surely not," I soothed her. "They're only looking out for you. Besides, ten is great in other ways."

"How so?"

"Well, first of all, people bring you bags of candy," I told her, gesturing toward myself with a thumb.

Sophia laughed. "That is fun," she conceded.

"The toys are fantastic too," I added.

"True," she agreed.

"Plus, and trust me on this, your friends are never as fun as when you're ten years old. Every time is a grand time!"

Sophia looked at me with fresh eyes. "I do have loads of fun with my friends."

"See? The world's your oyster, Sophia," I told her when we reached the kitchen.

"Here," Oliver said, standing and helping me to my chair.

"Thank you," I told him.

Eleanor watched us with keen eyes and I felt acutely aware of myself. I tried to see us as she saw us and guessed as to what she probably alleged. Her son had brought a girl home. The first since his wife had died. My heart plummeted to my feet as Oli scooted my chair in for me. I looked up at him, into his deep green eyes, memorizing his dark hair and gorgeous smile. My stomach flipped over and over. I tried to ignore it, but it wouldn't let me be.

During dinner, we discussed the weather and what our plans were for the next day. Oliver told everyone he'd planned on taking me into the village for a few hours to show me around, and inquired that afterward maybe we could all meet up for dinner.

"So where exactly are you from?" Eleanor asked when we were finished eating.

"I'm from Dallas, Texas."

"*Dallas!* Oh, I do love that show," she said. "They just don't make them like that anymore."

I giggled to myself. "They really don't," I told her.

"Weren't you in Dallas for a few weeks?" Zoe asked Oliver. "Oh! Is that where you and Oliver became acquainted?" Zoe asked me without waiting for his answer.

"It is," Oliver confirmed for me and set down his fork.

He looked over and smiled. "I'd actually pointed her out to Graham," he said to everyone. I thought he'd be done there, but he continued. "I remember it vividly. I pointed her out to him and said, 'That has got to be the most beautiful woman I have ever seen.'"

My heart hammered in my chest. "You didn't," I whispered.

The table got really quiet, including the baby, who must have read something in the atmosphere. She watched us intently. "I did, and Graham said he'd noticed you too and asked if he could have dibs."

"What'd you do that for?" George asked.

"It was Graham," Oliver explained.

Eleanor scoffed. "I've never liked him," she said. Then, realizing what she'd said, turned to me. "I'm sorry," she stammered.

I laughed and patted her hand. "No worries. I don't like him at all either, so we're on the same page there."

She relaxed. "He's just not a good boy," she told me. "I've never liked how he treats Oliver. He takes advantage."

Oliver sighed but didn't defend Graham or himself.

"What happened between you and Graham?" Sophia asked.

"Soph!" Zoe exclaimed.

"It's okay. He went out with another girl," I told Sophia, sticking to the kid-safe version of that explanation.

"He cheated!" Sophia shouted. "That is *so* wrong!" she exclaimed with ten-year-old vehemence. It made me smile.

"What a prat," Archie said into his plate.

"Archie!" Zoe yelled. "Arthur, these children!"

Arthur laughed. "Nothing to do with me."

So wrong, I mouthed to Sophia.

She folded her arms and pursed her lips then shook her head in disappointment. She looked straight at her uncle. "You don't need friends like that," she told him.

My hand went to my mouth to keep from laughing.

"Sophia," he pleaded, "this is just how men are. We don't kill friendships even when those friends act like idiots."

"Wrong," Sophia said, waving her little finger. "That's wrong, Uncle Oli. Wrong."

George was red in the face, keeping himself from laughing. So was Eleanor.

"Sophia," Oli said, a fit of laughter bubbling up from his throat. "You shouldn't talk to me that way."

"I'm sorry," Sophia apologized, realizing it might have been a little disrespectful, "but I think you should let go of that friend of yours."

"I'll think about it," Oli lied to appease her.

He looked at me and I shrugged my shoulders. "From the mouths of babes."

Chapter
Twelve

That night I'd had trouble sleeping, and it wasn't because I was in an unfamiliar house. I was always one of those who could adjust easily to a new surrounding. No, it was what Oliver had said at dinner. *That has got to be the most beautiful woman I have ever seen.* His declaration had skipped over my skin with a shudder and continued to dance for hours.

The next day, Oliver took me into Bray Village. I had trouble looking him in the eye. He was too good looking for me not to be affected by him. I didn't want to be any more confused than I had to be.

"There are only four three-Michelin-star restaurants in the United Kingdom, and two of them are here in this village."

"Shut the front door! That's so fancy!"

He snorted. "You slay me, Pen." He mocked my accent. "That's so fancee!"

I laughed. "Stop. It's hard living among the English accent with a Texas one, no matter how mild it is."

"Why? It fits you so well, Pen. I love to hear you talk."

Another pang of satisfying shivers swam through my body at his admission. I attached my phone to his car jack and searched for a song, something loud, something distracting. I scrolled through until I hit Imogen Heap's "Between Sheets" and hit play, but it didn't help. The melody was too heady and filled the car with an angst I wasn't yet ready to face.

We both reached the volume knob at the same time and our hands accidentally touched. His fingers on mine sent my thoughts and blood racing. My stomach rose to my head then fell back down in quick succession over and over, like a roller coaster without the bar fastened. It was thrilling, unbelievably thrilling. A thrill I'd never once experienced with Graham or anyone else.

I whipped my hand back.

"Sorry," he whispered, avoiding eye contact and staring straight ahead.

The car was quiet save for the building music. The crescendo of the song matched my steadily climbing heart rate.

I turned my head slowly toward Oliver. He glanced at me from the corner of his eye every few seconds, and each time I would turn quickly back toward the windshield. A sort of cat-and-mouse game that made me tingle all over.

Oliver's left hand went to the thigh of his jeans and I watched the movement closely. He wiped the palm of his hand down to his knee then brought his elbow to rest on the center console, letting his hand fall as close to me as possible without actually touching.

I swallowed. The proximity of his hand sent my head

spinning. My own good hand gripped the armrest, my knuckles white with the pressure of my grasp. I kept ordering myself to relax, to calm down, but no matter how hard I tried, it wasn't happening. My hand itched to touch his. I lifted it and made a small movement toward him, then I came to my senses and let it drop in my lap. Restless, I brought it to my hair and began to twist a strand around a finger over and over.

I felt Oliver's eyes on me, heavy. Heavier than I'd ever felt a stare, too physical, too visceral. I entertained myself, or if I was being truthful, diverted my attention from Oliver, by going over how awful an idea it would be to act on anything with him. He was Graham's best friend. Did I want to be the kind of girl who did something like that? Did I want to be *that* girl? Was I over Graham enough to give Oliver a fair chance? Did I like Oliver? Respect Oliver? Could I fall in love with Oliver?

My throat dry, I swallowed once more, and glimpsed at him.

Yes, my brain automatically replied.

No, you don't, Penelope. You don't. Stop, Penelope. Stop.

It was all moving so fast, too fast. I brought the side of my thumb to my mouth and chewed at the nail, something my mama never let me do. Remembering her, I let my hand fall back down.

"Something wrong?" Oliver asked from his side of the car.

I jumped slightly and laughed, sounding a little insane. "Uh, yeah? Why?" I asked, my eyes wide. *Oh my God, he knows. He can tell!*

"You seem a little jumpy."

"Jumpy?" I asked, trying to keep my body as still as

possible. "No, no. Not jumpy."

His brows pinched together and he fought a smile. "Why are you sitting like a statue now, then?" he asked.

We parked and he turned off the car. It fell silent. His hand rested on the door handle, but he wasn't getting out, he was staring at me.

My hand went to my face. "I'm an idiot is all. Carry on," I told him.

He got out and retrieved my scooter for me then met me on my side of the car.

"Your chariot awaits," he said, grabbing my hand.

Why do you have to be so charming?

He helped me onto the raised sidewalks and we strolled from shop to shop, always close enough to touch, but not actually touching, save for the occasional and accidental bump into one another. I found myself longing for those as the day progressed, and it was starting to scare me.

We'd made plans to meet up with his family at one of the local pubs for dinner and had an hour to kill. I'd expressed an interest in visiting an antiques shop because I'd grown fascinated by English teacups and had started collecting them since I'd first come over. Oliver found a gorgeous shop near the pub and we looked around. I eyed a blue flowery set with a petal saucer and stemmed cup. I hemmed and hawed over buying it in my mind, but ultimately decided it was just a little out of my price range, so I set it down and moved on to the next.

Oliver had gone off on his own, and I found myself loathing the distance. *Come on, Penny. Calm the hell down! This is Oliver. Oliver. Oliver, sleep-with-anything-that-moves Oliver.*

The memories of all the girls I'd seen him go home with poured a bucket of ice water over me like nothing else could. When Oliver found me again, I felt more like myself again. I smiled at him.

"Ready for dinner?" he asked when we met up.

"Ready," I told him.

He lifted a bag in front of me. "For you," he said.

"You bought me something?"

I took the bag. Inside was a small box. I stuck my hand in and peeled up the lid.

"You so obviously wanted it. I couldn't let you walk out of here without it," he told me.

It was the little teacup I'd admired when I thought he wasn't looking.

Uh-oh.

Chapter Thirteen

We met up with Oliver's family at the local pub and since we were fashionably late, most of them had already arrived. All, actually, except for Arthur.

"He's at the office," Zoe explained, buckling Imogen into her high chair.

Oliver pulled my chair out for me and I sat. "What does he do?" I asked.

"He's a barrister in London," Oliver explained.

"He should be here soon, though," Eleanor said. "So," she said, eyeing my bag. "What fabulous thing have you purchased in our little village?"

"Oh," I said, bringing up the bag and taking out Oli's gift. "Oliver bought it for me. I collect them."

"Oh, that's lovely!" Eleanor exclaimed. She picked up the cup and examined it from all sides. "Just gorgeous, darling. Good on you, Oliver. A very sweet gift," she told her son.

Oliver beamed with pride at his mom and my stomach flip-flopped again.

Everyone at the table took turns gushing over Oliver's gift, and I found myself delighted by his reaction to all their praises. He reminded me of a little boy who'd won a soccer tournament or something. I could see myself becoming infatuated with him, could feel it. The anxiety that gave me was palpable.

Dinner was wonderful, certainly nothing like the pub meals I was used to. It felt more like a restaurant experience than a pub experience. The boys retreated to the bar and had a few pints while the ladies talked. I played with Imogen and Sophia. Archie stuck by his dad's side, playing some kind of game on his phone.

"I've been meaning to ask you," Eleanor began, "how do you like London?"

I ran my fingers over the soft skin of Imogen's hand. "It's been amazing," I told them, which wasn't a lie. I added a caveat. "Everything but what's happened with Graham and me, that is." I laughed to break any tension I might have caused.

"Yes," Zoe agreed sweetly, patting my hand. "I'm sorry he did that to you, love."

Eleanor nodded her head then asked, "Penelope, dear, do you think you will *stay* in London?"

A sardonic brow raised on Zoe's face. "Mum, what are you playing at?"

"Nothing," Eleanor sang innocently. "I was just wondering if London could be a place she'd ever consider calling home, is all."

"I'm not sure," I told her honestly. "As cliché as it sounds, home is wherever my heart is. If my heart was in London, there would be my home."

Eleanor's face grew a little smug smile as she stared

down the tip of her nose at her daughter, who only rolled her eyes at her. *Had I really just said that?* Both Zoe and Eleanor were staring at me prospectively.

"When I'm older, I'm to move to London," Sophia chimed in, brushing the hair of one of her Barbies. I was grateful to her. She took the heat off.

"Oh, *are* you?" Zoe asked.

I signaled for Zoe to place Imogen in my lap and she did so. I kissed her baby cheek.

"Yes," Sophia confirmed, "I'll have a smashing time bumping around the city. I'll go to all the fancy restaurants and see all the shows."

"And the ballet," I added.

"Oh yes! The ballet, of course."

"You could live with Uncle Oliver," I told her.

"Oh no, no, no," she cooed. She set her tiny brush down on the table and started to braid her doll's hair. "I'll have a great big flat so my friends and I could have sleepovers."

"Naturally," I agreed with a nod.

My phone buzzed, indicating an email. "Excuse me, ladies," I told the women and glided on my scooter toward the entrance of the pub. I rolled outside and stood in the sun. I'd gotten a little chilly inside and used the excuse of checking my phone to come out into warmer air.

I unlocked it and checked my latest email.

From: Kaley Skarsgård <KSkarsgard@FACECosmetics.com>
    Subject: Advertising Opportunities
        Date: March 18, 2016 11:03:50 AM EDT
            To: Penelope Beckett <Penelope@PenelopeBeckett.com>

Miss Beckett,

I represent FACE Cosmetics in New York. We ran across your blog and were wondering if you'd be open to us advertising with you? We thought a few beginning vlog ads as well as dynamic ads on the blog itself. We were also wondering if you'd be interested in pulling together a vlog using our brand that has viral potential.

Please get back to me at your earliest convenience if you are interested.

Thanks so much,
Kaley Skarsgård
Advertising Executive for FACE Cosmetics

Holy. Cannoli. FACE Cosmetics was only the fastest rising makeup company in the United States. Was I interested? Hmm, let me think. Yes, I was interested!

I did a little shimmy as best I could in my casts and turned my scooter around just in time to run into Oliver.

"Oli! Oli!" I practically screamed.

"What's wrong?" he asked.

"Nothing! Oh my God, it's so amazing. I just got an email from FACE Cosmetics in New York and they want to advertise with me! Can you believe it?"

Oliver's face split into the biggest grin. "Yes, Pen, I can believe it. Such fantastic news!" he said, kissing my cheek. I found myself leaning forward as he dragged himself away and wishing he'd kept his lips on my skin for just a moment longer. "Come on, let's share it with everyone. Have a bit of a party since we're already here."

Feeling a bit drugged in the moment because Oliver kept his hand on my lower back, we made our way to his family's table. We spread my potential good news amongst ourselves and ordered celebratory pints for the adults and ice cream for the kids.

Eventually the pub started to fill in with a night crowd and Zoe and Arthur took their three sleepy kids home. George and Eleanor, Oli and I, moved to a booth and chatted for an hour before they too grew tired and left us to our own devices.

Oliver helped me type up a response to FACE. He insisted I include in my response that I was entertaining several offers and my rates were getting competitive. He promised me it was all part of the art of the negotiation and wouldn't let me take it out. He assured me it would work and that I needed to calm down when I kind of panicked after hitting the send button.

So when the cocktail waitress rounded our table, Oli ordered a shot for each of us and a pint chaser, which we drank quickly. Music pumped through the speakers above and a dozen of the locals had made a makeshift dance floor between several tables and were dancing.

"Right. We have to do that," Oli said, pointing at the dancers.

I laughed. "Oliver," I said, holding up my arm cast.

"No worries," he said, shifting out of his seat and stepping to my side of the booth.

Without preamble, he picked me up, tucking his arms under my knees and back as he always did. Surprised, I let out a little squeal and we both laughed. I wrapped my good hand around his neck and he held me a little tighter than usual. I could only assume the shot had given him a little bit of liquid courage and, goodness help me, I think the same made me let him do it.

Uh-oh.

When we reached the area with the other slow dancers, he let my body slide down his.

"Trust me?" he whispered.

"Of course," I answered.

He wrapped his arms around my waist and pressed

125

me close. My legs dangled beside his. We smiled at one another, but they dissipated. He swallowed and I followed the line of his throat.

Uh-oh.

"Penelope," his deep voice grated.

My good arm was folded at the elbow and my hand rested on a broad shoulder. He stared at me, something desperate in the look, and I knew what he was about to do.

"Let's not do this. Please, let's not do this," I begged.

"I have to. I need to," his pained voice expressed.

"He's your best friend," I whispered.

"I know," he agreed.

"I can't be that girl."

"*What* girl?" he asked, resting his cheek against mine and whispering in my ear. I felt his five o'clock shadow and tried to ignore how it made my heart speed up.

"*That* girl."

"You wouldn't be," he said.

"I would be, though. Don't you see?" I asked. I pushed at his shoulder a little and he let me slide down his lean, tall body once more until I gained some footing on my good leg. "I wouldn't just be the girl who went from one friend to another. I'd also be the *next* girl. Another notch on Oliver Finn's bedpost. You'd sleep with me once and grow tired of me just like all the others. I can't be that girl, Oliver. I'm not that girl. And as much as I like you, respect you in so many other ways." I swallowed and my eyes burned. "As much as I find you attractive, as much as you seem ideal, as much as I love calling you friend, I won't be the girl who tumbles around your group. I'm better than that," I told him.

I broke away from him and limped toward our table. I grabbed my canvas satchel and made my way toward the pub's exit. I didn't have a plan. I just needed space, needed air.

Oliver caught up with me, grabbing me by the elbow. "Penelope," he said, out of breath. "Wait. Please, wait."

"I think I've made a terrible mistake," I told him.

"No," he said. "No, you haven't. You're right. You are better than that. You're better than me, better than *Graham*. If you just stay a moment, let me pay the tab and I'll get us out of here. We'll talk or not. Whatever you want."

I nodded and stayed where I stood while he ran in and paid the tab. A few minutes later we walked silently to his car. He helped me inside and we drove back to his parents' house. Trying to seem as casual as possible, we both gathered our things and said our goodbyes. Eleanor looked a little panicked, but I tried to appease her by being as warm as possible. I don't think it fooled her one bit.

We left for London and drove the distance in silence. I hated the change in dynamics, detested it. I felt abandoned all over again. Justified or not, it was how I felt. The loneliness was overpowering.

"We never should have talked of it. If we'd kept silent, we'd be okay," I told the passenger side window.

"A lie," he said, cutting me deep. "I've been quiet for too long. My only regret is I did it too soon. You weren't ready to hear what I had to say. You still aren't, but now it's too late."

"I don't believe in regrets," I told him.

"You don't, but you're going to believe in mine, Pen,

because you don't have a choice." He turned into his garage and parked, whipping his head my direction. "You were supposed to be mine. From the beginning, you were supposed to be with *me*," he said, shocking me. "After giving in to Graham, you were an *immediate* regret. I should have *never* let him near you. I should have fought him tooth and nail for you, stranger or not, and now I am paying for that in unspeakable ways.

"Do you know what it was like to see him hold you, touch you, and *kiss* you?" His hands went to his hair and he tugged. "It's fucking *torture*! Every time I witnessed his hand graze your skin, his lips touch your lips. Every time he'd run his hand down your hair, hair I'd only dreamt of touching, it was excruciating.

"When the nurse called me that day from the hospital? I had to pull over twice to vomit. I raced through London to get to you. I must have lost five years off my life. I imagined the worst. Seeing you lay there hurt, finding out what Graham had done, I knew *I* had been the one who'd made the mistake. I knew I should have revealed myself to you that first day, but loyalty won out and what did it get me? Eight months of torment. I waited for you to leave him, waited for you to see what a terrible person Graham was to women, but time went by and you fell in love with him and I watched it happen and it was pure anguish, because as you fell for him, *I* fell for you.

"I've wanted you for so long. And that's the terrible part, Pen. For you, this is sudden. For you, this is but days. For me, though? For me, it's been eight months of trying to forget you, trying to move on, trying not to dream, to think, to want you."

His chest panted from the acknowledgment. He looked at me, expecting something, but I was struck speechless.

"Why didn't you tell me?" I asked, feeling incensed.

"It wasn't my place to break you up!"

"You knew what he was and you let me make the mistake!"

"It was not my place!" he yelled.

"You let me fall in love with the wrong guy!"

"You were supposed to see him for what he was. You were never supposed to love him."

The tears started streaming. "That's an issue, Oliver, you know why? Because I did fall in love, but it was the version of him he wanted me to love. It's the most damaging consequence associated with sociopaths. You love the person they want you to love, and then you're left with the aftermath when they finally decide to show their true colors. You could have spared me that, but your gosh damn loyalty to that snake in the grass overpowered these so-called feelings you hold for me!"

"Are you questioning me?" He looked offended, but I didn't have time for offended.

Because I was pissed, I didn't respond. I let my answer hang in the air.

"You think I don't want you?"

"Look at your patterns, Oliver. You sleep with every girl who will look at you. You claim that you've liked me from the beginning but let Graham *have* me," I bit out. "I don't really think you want me, not really. I think you want what you gave up. I think you want the closure, the triumph, the victory. Now I'm expected to believe that your yearning for me is sincere?"

129

"Bullshit!" he shouted. "That's bullshit," he said again, quieter. He grabbed my shoulder and brought me closer to him. "You *know* it is." He searched my face for something. "You felt something these past few days. I didn't imagine the searing chemistry between the two of us. You can lie to yourself, but you can't lie to me."

I refused to acknowledge how right his words were. "Answer for yourself, then," I said instead.

"For what!"

"Have you struggled these last eight months because it's actually me you want, or was it the missed opportunity for another conquest?"

"I want you," he said without hesitation. The heated, searing declaration melted me to my seat.

"I-I don't believe you," I lied. I did believe him, but I couldn't let it go. Things had gotten too complicated and I needed an out. *Don't hurt him like that, though.*

His shoulders sagged, and I regretted my words immediately. He opened his door and climbed out. He came to my side and helped me from the car but wouldn't look at me.

"Oli," I said, hoping to apologize, my head swimming.

"Don't," he insisted. "Don't, Penelope."

In an instant he went from hot to cold.

"Listen to me," I told him, hoping to talk further.

"Penelope!" he shouted, his voice echoing off the walls.

I clenched my jaw shut and scrambled up the stairs to the metal door. I waited for him to open it and moved aside when he entered first. He tried to help me over the slight hitch between the door and the floor, but I wouldn't let him. I headed for my room and closed the door behind me.

I packed all my stuff as quickly as possible and sprinted as fast as my cast would allow toward the garage door and opened it, tossing everything I had down the steps, hobbling after it and booking it toward street level, waiting at the curb for a passing taxi.

"Please, please," I whispered, praying for one to pass by.

"Penelope!" I heard from the garage.

"Shit," I whispered toward the street.

"Pen! What are you doing?" Oliver asked.

"Just let me go, Oliver," I pleaded as a taxi pulled around the corner. I shot my hand out for him and he pulled up beside me.

"You are not fucking leaving right now," he said, hitting the top of the taxi, signaling for the driver to keep going.

The driver drove away, looking for another rider.

I stuck out my hand again. "What the hell, Oliver?"

"Come back inside," he asked softly.

I shook my head. "It's all a little too much to take, for me to take."

"I understand," he said, "but let's not jump the gun here."

"Graham ripped my heart to shreds." He nodded. "I'm not healed enough to look at you the way my heart wants me to. And, to be honest, neither are you." A look of disappointment flashed across his face. "You need to deal with the heartache Brooke caused that still lies at your feet." He bit his bottom lip and looked away from me. Another taxi pulled next to me and the driver got out to put my bags inside. "I lied before," I told him. "I know it's

131

me you want. Know it's you I want too, but there's a canyon between us neither of us are ready to vault over. Neither of us would survive it."

Oliver's jaw gritted. I reached for it and smoothed my thumb across his cheek. The muscle relaxed and he turned his face into my palm. I pulled him down and placed a firm, trembling kiss on his mouth. Altogether too soon, I forced myself to push away and sat in the taxi. We took off and I refused to look back because that brief brush of our lips did more for me than a thousand passionate kisses from his best friend. If I'd let my eyes meet his, I wouldn't have left.

And I needed to leave, because Oliver had been right. I *had* changed for Graham. It was time for me to find myself again and hope I was still there.

Chapter Fourteen

6 Months Later...

Bargain
[**Bahr**-g*uh* n]
noun
1. An agreement between parties settling what each shall give and take or perform and receive in a transaction.

Penelope Beckett offers whatever it takes to get things back to what they were, even and often, her dignity.

I shoved the key in my London flat's lock and opened the door, pushing the mountain of mail that had slipped through the slot in my door onto the floor. My business landline was ringing so I raced to catch it, ignoring the slight wince of pain I still felt in my healed leg.

"Penelope Beckett!" I answered.

"Penelope, it's Georgiana from FACE London."

"How many Georgianas do you think I know?" I teased her. "How are you?" I asked.

"I'm well except I've had the toughest time reaching you! Where have you been?"

"I took a week off to visit home."

"Right. Good on you. Did you have a lovely time?"

"It was awesome to see my family again, yeah, but good to be back home."

Home.

"Wonderful! And so good to hear, because I have another proposition for you. As you know London Fashion Week is approaching on the sixteenth and FACE wants you to be the, no pun intended, face of our campaign."

I was flattered and a little flabbergasted. "Georgiana, let me just sit down for a minute," I begged and fell into my rolling desk chair. "You want me to be the face of FACE's campaign for fashion week?"

"Yes, darling! What do you say?"

"I say yes! Are you kidding?"

"Good, sweetheart. We like how fast you've been growing, your reach, and we love your face, darling. I think it's such a fab idea. We've known for days, and we were dying to tell you!"

"Thank you, Georgiana, this is fantastic news. I'm so honored."

"Brilliant! I'll send the contracts over soon. Have a look at them and I'll see you on Thursday?"

"Thursday then. Bye, Georgiana."

"Cheers, darling!"

I hung up the phone and swirled around in my chair, beyond giddy. My first inclination was to text Oliver, but I set my phone down, ignoring the pain in my chest I always got when I thought of him. I'd gotten over Graham tolerably well. Never thought of the (Picking up the vernacular ;) —>) sodding bastard, to be honest, but Oliver was different. I still thought of Oliver daily and wondered what he was up to.

Every now and again I would google him or Finn Leathers and read up on what he was up to. He took my advice and built a better online presence. I even noticed he'd published the rough commercial I had shot for him. I checked out the Zoe bag when I saw it was available for purchase and was floored to see during the past six months that the price had gone from a staggering six thousand pounds to a whopping twenty thousand, which meant the bag was in demand and was doing well. I'd seen several celebrities photographed with it in the tabloids and was happy for him.

My heart sank a little imagining Oliver at his workbench, churning out his masterpieces and no one really knowing what all went into making them. So many times after I had left him that day, I longed to show up on his doorstep unannounced, but pride and a little bit of common sense reeled me back in.

Tears pricked my eyes. "God, if you just give me back a little bit of peace, I promise to try and stop thinking about him."

I jumped up, determined not to let myself get down. I walked into my galley kitchen and went straight for the fridge, grabbing yet another bottle of water, my fifth for the day. Downing water was a coping mechanism for me, kept the hands busy. My skin had never looked better.

I had a sweet little flat. I'd bought it in cash with the

proceeds of the first viral ads I'd done for FACE, the offer I'd gotten while at that pub in Bray with Oliver. His tactic had worked and they offered double what was considered standard.

That viral advertisement had rocketed me forward and I got so many offers for more, I actually had the option of being choosy for a change. I'd often wondered if Oli had seen that first vid and what he thought of it.

I'd decided to stay in London because I loved the city. I'd remembered something Oliver had told me about living for the adventure, but I was also staying because of what I'd said to his mother about wherever my heart wanted to be would be my home. And my heart was in London. It didn't belong to anyone, not really, but it did wander the streets every now and again hoping to spot its mate. I wouldn't argue with it. It felt right in London. I knew that could change, but for the moment, I was going to go with my gut. For six months, I figured myself out, discovered who I was, and remembered why I liked being me. London had helped me do that.

I'd gotten on well with a downstairs neighbor named Claire who'd introduced herself to me the first day, and we'd bounced around the city together often. She was an import as well, but from not quite as far. Manchester, actually, and since she was fairly new to the area, she didn't know anyone either, which made me feel a heck of a lot less lonely. She traveled so often for work, though, that our meetups were sporadic at best. I found myself going out most nights with the girls who worked at FACE, who were wonderful in their own right, but a little too rambunctious for my taste. I could barely keep up, to be honest. Quintessential "Oh-my-gawd!" girls, if you catch my drift. They were great when I wanted a few hours of wild, but I would break off from them most early mornings and retreat to my place to bask in the quiet, which was a reprieve, let me tell you. I really did have a sweet little flat. Full of books. Lots and lots of shelves full of lots and lots of books. Sigh.

Several days after Georgiana sent over the contracts and my attorney had gone over the terms, I signed them and had them couriered over just in time for the first photo shoot the next day, which I had every intention of documenting for several upcoming vlogs I had coming up for a fashion week blitz. I was stoked. I fought yet another urge to text Oliver and tell him my good news.

I found myself often asking God if He would consider taking my pain away in a swap for many other things when I was getting over the fictitious version of Graham I had fallen in love with. But it quickly graduated into bargaining for a reprieve from the hole I felt when I thought of Oliver, which brought that sharp chest pain back with the added exception that it felt even more acute when I thought of Oli, despite having only really considered him for a few days and in the wake of Graham.

It was the way he'd talked to me, treated me, looked at me that had done things to my insides. Things that felt irreversible and eventually it was everything I could do to get the reminders of him to dissipate. Thus, the bargaining with God. It was what it was.

I looked at the mountain of mail at my door for the millionth time since coming home. I sighed at the ginormous task of it all. There were several hundred envelopes as well as at least ten large and medium boxes, which meant Claire had dropped those in with the spare

I'd left her. I reminded myself to get her a thank-you gift.

I tackled the stacks one by one. Most were spam mail, which got tossed into recycling. There was my vlog mail that my sister-in-law forwarded from my PO Box back in Dallas. Then there was a small stack of personal letters, which I found odd, since everyone I knew in London besides the oh-my-gawd girls from FACE and Claire were speaking to me, negating the need to write. I set those aside and opened the boxes first because, let's face it, those were the fun ones.

One box held brushes from a cosmetics company that was probably hoping I'd review them online. Another was a complete shadow set from an exclusive and large company that was flirting with the idea of advertising with me. I worked it out in my head that it was probably a test. It didn't matter to me. I was going to pass with flying colors, or flying shadows, that is. What! What! I got several more boxes full of product I was dying to try. If I got it for free, I would most likely review them, that was the deal. I was always looking for things to blog about it, so product landing at my door was fine with me. Occasionally they wouldn't like the results of my tests, but I wasn't going to sugarcoat it to my viewers. They trusted me, and I wasn't going to steer them wrong.

I saved the biggest box for last because I wanted to save the best for last, at least I hoped it would be the best. Giddy, I ran a butter knife over the taped closure and pulled at the ends. Inside was another box, a crisper box, *wrapped with twine.*

"Oh my gosh," I whispered, my heart racing.

I yanked out the twined box and set it on top of my dining table. "Oh my gosh," I said again. "Oh my gosh."

I cut the twine and pried open the lid. My stomach dropped to my feet when I saw the blue velvet case. Reverently, I pulled out the large case and set it down onto the table. I tugged the edges down to reveal one of Oliver's Zoe bags.

Adrenaline pumped through my veins. "Oh my gosh." With trembling fingers, I picked up the bag and examined the work. I didn't know how, but I'd forgotten how well made the bag was. It was utterly pristine. I ran my fingers over the craftsmanship, imagined how Oliver's hands must have done the same when he'd inspected his work.

I opened the top and peeked inside. There was a notecard in an envelope setting at the bottom of the bag with my name handwritten on its face. My heart thumped wildly in my chest. My hands shook as they reached for the note and pulled it out. There was a wax seal over the fold and I studied the imprint. It was the letter F with the year 1509 beneath it. My finger ran over the mark, and my heart skipped a beat. Keeping the seal intact, I tugged open the envelope and pulled out the note.

Pen,
This is the original. I couldn't sell it because it belongs to you.
The success I've had from it was all your doing.

-Oliver Finn

My hands went to my face and came away wet. I sighed. My arms wrapped around the bag like it was a lifeline to him. I fell into a dining chair and sat there for several minutes, stunned. I stood. Then sat. Then stood.

"Do I call him?" I asked myself. I sat. "No, send him a thank you?" I stood. "No, too impersonal," I argued with myself then sat again.

I tried to psych myself up to call him. I toggled back and forth between phoning and actually showing up at his door, but knew that would look too desperate.

"Shit, shit, shit!"

I knew what I had to do. *Don't hesitate.* I picked up my cell, found his contact, and hit send. *Shit, shit, shit!*

"Hello?" a young woman's voice answered, throwing me off.

"Uh, um," I stuttered. "Is this Oliver Finn's number?"

"*Who* is *this*?" she asked territorially.

Shit, shit, shit! "So sorry, it's a business matter. Sorry to disturb you," I apologized like an ass.

I quickly hung up, feeling like an absolute idiot. Right, calling was a bad idea, a very bad idea. My phone buzzed on my table and I practically jumped to the ceiling. The ID read his name and I hit end. No way was I going to talk to whomever she was, but I knew I did need to thank him.

My hand found the leather of the bag again. I gathered my purse from the chair next to me and transferred all my stuff to the Zoe. Next, I turned the cameras on in my little studio study and recorded a quick vlog on Oli's gift, dropping the links for those who wanted to purchase one for themselves at the bottom of the video. I gushed over the beauty of the bag, the quality, and how much I loved it. I sent him a warm thank you and the link to the video after it was edited by email, hoping the gesture let him know how much I appreciated his gift.

I turned off my computer and cameras as well as my

phone and went to bed. I had the photo shoot the next day and wanted to look well rested. I laid the Zoe bag on its own pillow and stared at it until I dozed off.

I dreamed of Oliver that night.

 Chapter
Fifteen

I was scheduled to be at FACE at five in the morning, which is a freaking beating, but apparently they wanted to catch the sunrise light. I stumbled into the studio with wet hair and a fresh, clean face. When I arrived, Georgiana handed me a hot cup of coffee.

"What in the world, Georgiana?" I grated, practically yanking the cup from her hand.

"I know," her gorgeous voice told me. Her words sounded annoyed but her face looked flawless, which really irked me.

"How?" I asked her, gesturing to her perfect face. "How is that face possible at five a.m.?"

"I don't know what you're talking about," she lied.

"I just rolled out of bed like this, dearie," I mocked with an ever-improving English accent, if I said so myself. "I really didn't do anything. I'm *that* perfect."

She laughed. "Do us a favor, love. Drink your coffee and don't talk to us until after you've finished."

I snorted and laughed, which I'm sure was attractive.

"I bet you're rethinking your offer," I teased. "But too late! The contracts are signed. You're stuck!"

"Hush," she said, slapping me on the butt a little to get me going.

I laughed as I approached hair and makeup. "Good morning, you wonderful people! Make me dazzle!" I told them, sitting in the chair.

For two hours I sat in that chair and my bum grew impossibly numb. I had to force them twice to let me up to walk around a bit to get some circulation back there again, but when all was said and done, I discovered why FACE was the fastest growing cosmetics company in the United States as well as the United Kingdom.

"It's pretty spectacular," Georgiana told me over my shoulder when they were done. "I believe we've made a fantastic choice," she told me.

"Thank you, Georgiana. I'm living a dream, it seems, and having a blast while I do it. I'm going to enjoy it while it lasts."

"Something tells me you'll last for quite some time," she said, pinching my shoulder gently. Her eyes shifted to my bag setting on a nearby chair. "Could you please tell me something, though?"

"What's that?" I asked.

"How the *bloody hell* did you get a Zoe bag when there is a two-year wait?"

My heart sped up into my throat. "There's a two-year wait?" I asked her.

"And growing," she said.

"That's incredible," I admitted.

"So?" she demanded.

"Oh, well, I know the maker, Oliver Finn, personally," I

hedged.

"Oh my God! Please tell me you can get me bumped up the list!" she begged, bouncing on her heels.

"Georgiana, if I could, I would, but our relationship is a precarious one. I wouldn't be able to get you up the list. I'm sorry." *Best to disappoint her now.*

The bag forgotten, her face lit up at my confession and she leaned into me. "Give me all the hellacious details, darling."

I was *not* about to do anything of the sort. I aimed for a version of the truth. "Well, I dated his best mate and now his mate and I aren't speaking so—" I said, leaving it open.

This explanation satisfied her. "Oh, impossible. That's too bad then." She peered over at the bag and sighed wistfully.

"Go on," I said. "Pick her up."

Georgiana did just that and swung her arm out. "Oh, bugger me. It's as soft as a baby's ass!"

"You're hopeless." I giggled.

"It's too bad you're not on the best of terms with the maker," Georgiana commented, something strange in her tone as she examined the seams.

"What? Why?" I asked.

"Well, he's going to be there next week."

I shot upright. "What!"

Georgiana eyed me strangely. I tried to check my reaction, though it felt a little late.

"Right," she said, examining me closer. "Well, he's meant to be at a few shows. Two designers commissioned a few bags from him and are showcasing them on their runways."

I gulped. "Wow, that's incredible." As casually as I could, I asked, "Do you know what shows?"

"Haven't the foggiest."

Well, that was the end of that. If I inquired any more forcefully, I'd have given myself away completely. I knew it didn't matter, though. That was what Google was for. The trouble with Georgiana inadvertently spilling information I was dying to know meant that the photo shoot had come and gone in a flash and I wasn't in the state of mind to truly enjoy it as I had wanted, too distracted with wanting to know what shows Oliver would be at, what he would wear, what he would look like, how he would smile, and what he would say if I ran into him.

Later at home, instead of editing my photo shoot video as I should have, I checked Oli's social accounts and searched for any sort of idea which shows he'd be at, but of course, Oliver didn't care about fashion week all that much. He had only made a single status update the week before, which read:

The Zoe bag will be featured at London Fashion Week, so that's cool.

Men. I spent two hours combing over each designer's website showing that week and eventually found both designers. The first show was on day one at Andy Marks's show and the second was on day four at Alice & Emma. My fingers shook as I typed the dates and times for each show into my phone's calendar. There was only one slight problem. I had a ticket for the Andy Marks's show but not for Alice & Emma's, and chances were slim I'd get one because of their popularity.

I texted Georgiana.

Looking for a ticket to Alice & Emma Thursday. Know where I can filch one?

I bit at the skin of my thumb while waiting for a reply.

Sorry, love. No such luck here, she wrote.

Damn. I was going to have to get creative.

During the next several days FACE London launched our campaign, and I worked endless hours promoting FACE on my blog and making tons of live videos of myself at random events they hosted. I was utterly exhausted by the following Sunday, yet I still had the worst time sleeping because I knew there was a chance I was going to see Oliver at Andy Marks's show the following Monday. My mind and my heart were too chaotic for rest.

Morning of the show, I woke groggy and feeling sick to my stomach. My nerves were my worst enemy. I decided a long, hot shower was in order. It helped tame the overpowering emotions coursing through my body. I wrapped my hair in a towel and stuffed into a short slip just as the doorbell rang.

I'd hired a hair and makeup artist to get me ready that morning knowing I would be filming a lot. When I peered through the peephole, Henry, my hair stylist, and Siena, a rep from FACE, were standing in the hall with their bags. I pulled it open for them and discovered Claire was also standing with them.

"Hello!" I greeted all three, kissing each of their cheeks as they entered.

I sat in my bathroom after setting up my cameras for another film segment and let them do their thing while Claire perused my closet.

"What are you wearing?" she asked.

"Not a clue!" I shouted toward her.

She sprinted into the bathroom with us. "You haven't bought something?"

"No!" I panicked. "I didn't have time. I haven't had a minute, Claire, I swear."

"Penelope." She groaned. "This isn't like you."

"I know," I agreed, wringing my hands. "I've been a little distracted lately."

"Well, I can see that," she soothed. "You've got a lot on your plate right now."

I didn't correct her misconception. The truth was it was Oliver who'd been my one true distraction. "So, what do you think?"

She sat at the edge of my sink and thought. Her face lit up and she snapped her fingers. "Got it. That navy silk one-piece jumper! It's perfect!"

I was hesitant. "I'm not sure," I said, thinking about how uncomfortable it usually got after a few hours.

"Oh, please!" she shouted, jumped up, and ran toward my room. Thirty seconds later she emerged with the jumper in question.

Henry and Siena urged me to try it on when they were done. I shoved them all out of the bathroom and tried it on. I'd had to edit changing from the tape. It was a beautiful piece, long sleeved, deep V-neckline. I shoved on the heels Claire had paired with them, but they seemed all wrong.

"Claire!" I shouted through the door.

"Yes, darling?"

"Grab those open-toed pumps, will you?"

I heard Claire open my wardrobe and laugh. "Which

ones?"

"Uh, they're camel leather, the back wraps up the heel and the ankle, and the front is open with small ties lacing up the front."

"Right. Found them," she said, opening the door and handing them over.

I replaced the heels she'd originally given me with the others and stood up. *Much better.*

"Henry, Siena, come look," Claire ordered, and they both emerged in the doorway. Siena gushed over the shoes.

"You look smashing, Penelope," Henry crooned.

"Really sexy, doll," Siena confirmed.

"Just brilliant!" Claire added for good measure, her hands clasped at her chest. "Take care you don't break too many hearts," she teased with a wink then smiled.

I studied myself in my mirror.

Oh, there was only one heart I wanted near that day. I just hoped he still wanted near mine.

Chapter Sixteen

After showing my guests out with a careful kiss apiece, I spritzed myself with the perfume I wore while I had lived with Oliver and had not worn since because it reminded me too much of him. Giddy with nerves and excitement, I grabbed my gifted bag and locked up my flat.

I timed my breathing to keep from passing out and headed for street level, signaling for a taxi. A few blocks from the event, the line of cars dropping off the odd celebrity was packed. Andy Marks's show was the third of the day, but the most important. My heart started to race as we neared the drop-off.

"Ticket, please," a man asked. He leaned into the window. He was wearing a fashion week T-shirt and a pair of headphones with a microphone and carried a clipboard with him.

I handed over my ticket and he flipped through sheets of paper to confirm my name.

"Penelope Beckett. You're with FACE London?"

"That's me."

He opened my door for me and I paid the driver.

"Right," the rep said, "so stay in this spot here. Someone will signal you when it's time to walk."

"Oh, okay. Thanks," I told him and congregated near three people I didn't recognize.

Two of them stood close together and glanced back at me, no doubt wondering who I was. *I'm a nobody,* I wanted to inform them, but kept my mouth shut. Another man with a fashion week T-shirt approached the couple ahead and signaled them to walk ahead. Cameras flashed incessantly their direction and my heart started to pound anew for a brand-new reason. I hadn't considered the paparazzi, my thoughts too preoccupied with other things.

Oh crap. I started breathing too quickly and had to force myself to slow down. *It's okay. It's okay.* The mantra ran through my mind. The woman in front of me moved forward.

"Penelope?" a deep voice called out behind me.

I turned around to see none other than *Oliver* stepping from his Range Rover and handing a set of keys to a valet. I nearly gasped. *Oh my God. Oh my God. Oh my God. Calm. Just calm down.* He was dressed impeccably, another one of his three-piece suits, his undercut slicked back. He'd grown a slight beard since I'd last seen him, but it was well kept, trimmed perfectly, and looked like the rest of him, groomed to an impeccable excellence. He was more handsome than I had ever seen him. My body melted right there on the spot.

I smiled at him and he smiled back. I expected him to walk my direction, but instead he turned back and and held out his palm. A tan hand found his and my stomach dropped to the cement below my feet. An unfair, equally gorgeous woman met his side. I wanted to slink away, to hide, and for some inexplicable reason cry until I had nothing left to shed. Instead, I stood tall and took a deep breath.

The woman had long blonde hair, wore a beautiful but too short dress, and her legs continued for miles. I was a good five foot ten with my heels on, but she reached six foot easily. She looked like she better belonged on the catwalk than the red carpet. My stomach flipped over and over when I saw how well they looked together.

I looked down at my thin gold chains and made sure they fell nicely down the V of my jumper. Tossing my hair back as subtly as possible, I lifted my head and met his eyes. My own stung with unshed tears as I took another deep breath to steady myself.

"Penelope, it's so good to see you," Oliver said.

"Hello, Oliver," was all I managed to eke out.

"Hello." He glanced down at my bag. "I see you got the bag."

It sat in the crook of my arm and I lifted it slightly then let it drop back down. "Oh my God, yes. Uh, um, thank you so much. W-words can't express," I fumbled out. *Apparently.* My cheeks burned.

Oliver smiled that clever smile of his, the one that let on he knew more than he was revealing. I realized how much I missed it.

"You're welcome. And thank you for the video. I got a hundred more orders after you posted it, and I'm sure I'll have a hundred more in my email when I get back."

"I hope you didn't find that too forward," I said

formally.

"Not at all. It was kind."

Oh my God! This is a disaster! We're talking like we've never met before.

Oliver stared at me as the blonde goddess met his side after talking with someone she'd run into. To avoid the heat of his incredible gaze, I turned toward his date. It was Oliver's turn to be awkward.

"I'm so sorry," he blurted, remembering himself. His hand rested at the small of her back, which made me feel ill. "This is Jasmine."

Jasmine stuck out her hand and I took it.

"Like the princess!" I stupidly babbled.

"Yes," she said with a smile that revealed she was out of my league, "just like." Her London accent coupled with the sexpot timbre of her voice was too much. I was growing smaller by the second next to her.

"Oh God," I muttered. "I'm an idiot. Sorry." My hand went to my hair and I sighed. "I'm sorry, Jasmine. I'm just a bit awkward." I pointed to my head. "No filter. It can't be helped, unfortunately," I chattered. Jasmine looked concerned, which sucked. "Just ignore me!" I giggled like a buffoon.

"Excuse me," I heard someone shout behind me.

I turned to find the assistant yelling my direction, for quite a while possibly, judging by the frustrated look on his face.

"Well, got to go. As you can see," I said, gesturing behind me. "See you inside?" I asked and shot off without waiting for an answer.

I wanted to die. I practically ran into the assistant, forcing him to catch me and set me to rights.

"Oh Lord, I'm sorry. Excuse me."

"You okay?" he asked.

"Yes, fine. Thanks. Where to?"

"Just this way. Don't forget to smile," he encouraged.

I gulped and breathed one deep breath before raising my face to the flash of cameras before me. I smiled and forced myself to forget the humiliating spectacle I'd just been the star of. I posed for the cameras and flirted with the photographers, letting them know who I was, what I did, and who I represented when they yelled their questions. The whole affair took less than ten minutes, but by the end I was exhausted. I wondered how celebrities did it so often without wanting to tear their hair out afterward. I wanted to find Georgiana. Hell, I'd have settled for an oh-my-gawd girl at that point.

Inside, it was packed to the max. The catwalk was lined with chairs already filled with celebrities I had no chance of getting anywhere near. I studied their faces and their bodies, a secret thrill that I was sharing air with them, then I realized something.

They were human. They're literally human like everyone else. Their faces weren't any more beautiful than a lot of people you saw walking down the street. Their bodies, while toned, really weren't anything you'd lend godhood to. I giggled to myself wondering how many people out there broke their backs to try to be like them. Little did they know they already were, save for the fame and possibly fortune part, but as we all know, neither of those things brings you happiness.

Rounding the edge of the crowd, I slunk toward the back hoping to get a glimpse of Georgiana. I finally found her in the corner two rows back from the right side of the catwalk. She saw me and waved me toward her. She pointed toward a seat next to her.

"Awesome!" I shouted over the din of the crowd at her with an "okay" signal.

I skirted past ten or so people who looked important, probably were important, but couldn't bring myself to care all that much because all I wanted to do was sit down and catalog all the stupid crap I'd done before walking the red carpet.

"How did it go?" Georgiana asked as I sat.

"Fine, I suppose. I chatted up the photographers, let them know I repped FACE. You'd have been so proud," I told her.

She squeezed my hand. "Oh, that's just brilliant, Penelope! I'm so getting a raise when all is said and done this week. And Pen?" she asked to get my attention. I turned toward her. "Your campaign has brought us such a kick in revenue, darling!"

"Get out of town! I'm so happy! What a success!"

"I know," she said, throwing out her hands. "The world is our oyster, Penelope Beckett!"

I laughed. "You are such a silly girl and I love it."

She sighed and laughed, wrapping her arm in mine. After a few minutes, she leaned into my ear. "Don't look now, but there is an incredible specimen across the catwalk from us who can't stop staring at you."

My heart leapt into my throat. "Directly across?" I whispered.

"Across and maybe three chairs to your left? Sharp hair. Shaggy beard. Cut body. Seriously gorgeous, darling."

My blood burned with adrenaline. "Oh my God, I think that's Oliver Finn."

"The bag guy?"

"The very one."

"Well, look then, but keep it casual."

I let my gaze wander toward the top of the catwalk and then as coolly as possible, let it swing in the direction Georgiana indicated. It *was* Oliver and he was staring directly at me, the heat of his gaze warming me up to an impossible temperature. I shifted in my seat. My necklace and bracelets jingled as I did so. I tossed my hair from side to side to get some ventilation then smiled and waved.

Instead of matching my smile as I expected, he kept his gaze serious. It burned me to a crisp on the inside. I felt Georgiana lean farther into me.

"Oh my God, Penny. That boy wants to eat you for dinner."

I felt my face flush. "No, he doesn't, George. Look at his date."

Georgiana giggled. "I guess *I* should since *he* can't seem to be bothered."

I broke the gaze somehow and turned into her. "I don't know why he keeps staring."

"You don't? I never mistook you for a fool, Penelope."

I laughed. "Hush."

Someone called her name from two rows up and she waved before standing and bending over the patrons behind us to speak to her acquaintance. I was forgotten. Turning back toward Oli, I raised my eyes to his.

How are you? he mouthed.

Hot, I mouthed back, fanning myself.

A sardonic brow raised as well as that Oliver smirk and I realized the double meaning. My face grew hotter as my hands found my cheeks. Oliver laughed, like really gut laughed, which caught the attention of Jasmine and she followed the line of his stare toward me. She sat upright when she saw who he was looking at. She arched her back, which pushed her chest out, then bent into his side. His hand went to her knee as she whispered something into his ear, and I felt my world crumble a little bit more. The tips of his fingers turned white with the grip of his hand, which made me feel sick to my stomach.

That hand could have been on your knee, I scolded myself. *But I wasn't ready,* I argued back like a lunatic. *And he's not into monogamy. No matter how well you carry on together, he will never be able to settle down with one girl.*

Convinced I'd made the right decision six months before as well as satisfied with the idea we could never really be more than what we'd been, I angled my body away from them, and made a pact with myself not to look their direction, no matter what.

The house lights dimmed over the audience and brightened over the runway. The crowd grew quiet.

"Show's on," Georgiana whispered.

Loud music pumped throughout the overhead speakers and I stole a glance their direction then immediately chided myself. Lines of girls appeared from behind the walls as Andy Marks's show commenced with flourish. I took at least a thousand pictures with the intent of putting them into a slideshow on the blog along with a few forced selfies with as many people as possible.

The girls kept coming, and I found myself enthralled with the collection. Lots of unusual prints in gorgeous fabrics flitted down the runway. The following spring was going to be beautiful if what I was looking at was any indication.

My skin felt heavy and uncomfortable, as if someone was watching me. My hand went to my throat and held there in an attempt to deflect, but it did no good. I tried to glimpse Oli again, but they had lowered the house lights on his side of the runway even more to bring further attention to the colors of the new fabrics flitting down on the models, I guessed.

I couldn't see him, but I could *feel* him. I couldn't hold it anymore and shivered all over. I heard the faintest laugh titter across the catwalk and blushed from head to toe.

Chapter
Seventeen

Outside of the show, it was impossible to get a taxi. I sat on a stone hedge outside the building and decided to wait for the crowd to thin out. Georgiana had offered me a ride, but we were going in opposite directions and I knew she would be late to her next show if she accommodated me.

"I'll see you tonight, then, darling. Seven?"

"Seven," I confirmed, kissing her cheek.

"Bye, love."

"Bye, babe."

I tried hard not to watch the crowds, tried hard not to search for Oliver's head, tried not to think of him in his suit, and clean shoes, with his perfect teeth, and crooked smile. I tried not to imagine his hand on Jasmine's knee, tried not to think of my knee there instead.

"Pen," I heard to my right. I jumped.

"Oliver!" I gasped.

"Did I scare you?" he asked.

"A-a little," I admitted, standing up.

I heard a rip when I did and stopped still. Oliver's mouth dropped open.

"Of course," I told the sky. I turned around at an uncomfortable angle and surveyed the damage. I had a long tear running down my right butt cheek and back-upper thigh. "Thank God I wore boy shorts under this!" I turned back around and faced a red-faced Oli, his hand at his mouth to hide his laugh. "You probably love this," I told him, fed up.

"I do not!" He laughed openly.

"Now I have to go home and change. I was supposed to go to that stupid luncheon at Preston's. I'll never get a taxi there and back in time."

"I'm headed there now. Why don't I take you to wherever you're staying and then to the luncheon?"

My throat went dry. "You're headed to Preston's?"

"That's what I said, Pen."

My heart raced. "It would be sort of inconvenient. I live on the outskirts."

Oliver looked shocked. "You still live in London?" he asked.

My brows pinched in confusion. "You didn't know?"

"I thought you'd gone back to Dallas. I thought you were only here for fashion week."

I swallowed. "No," I explained, "I never left London."

He looked like I'd socked him in the stomach. "You've been in this bloody town this whole time?"

I nodded.

He shook his head as if to clear it. "Right. Well, then we should hurry."

Adrenaline pumped through my veins at an alarming rate. "Okay, thank you."

"Just let me fetch Jasmine."

"Of course," I answered calmly but secretly died inside.

He left and I watched him drag Jasmine away from a conversation with a group of people. I watched him explain what was going on as they walked. She stopped and folded her arms.

"Oh shit," I whispered, not wanting to be the cause of a fight.

He placed a hand on her forearm and she relaxed, making me feel sick again, then they both came waltzing my direction like bloody Will and Kate, but swapped hair colors.

"I'm so sorry," I told Jasmine as she approached.

"It's fine," she told me, a saccharine smile on her lovely face.

She made me feel smaller than I'd ever felt in my entire life.

"This way," Oliver said, gesturing toward the valet.

We walked in silence save for a couple of whistles my direction that made me want to crawl beneath a bench. I pressed my Zoe bag against the gigantic hole in my jumper, but it still wasn't large enough. Needless to say, it was awkward beyond belief. I saw a taxi driving toward us and I almost shot my hand out for it. Then I thought of having to face them at Preston's. I'd reached my limit in acting like a jackass around them that day and decided to commit to the ride.

I waited as Oliver opened the door for Jasmine and she sat. He opened my door for me and I slid in sideways so I wouldn't flash him through my rip. Once Oliver was in, he started the engine and he pulled out, heading for the garage's exit.

"Where to, Pen?" he asked. The way he said my nickname made my heart jump into my throat.

"Uh, other side of the Thames," I told him then heard Jasmine sigh like she was exasperated. *Oh my God, this is awful.* I gave him the address and he plugged it into his navigation system.

It was quiet for a while until Oliver broke the silence. "Are you renting?" he asked conversationally.

"No," I told them, "I bought. Real estate in London can be a great investment."

"It is," he agreed. I couldn't read his facial expression but wished I could. Jasmine stayed quiet.

Somebody kill me.

"If you've bought then you must plan on staying awhile," he commented.

"Not sure, really. I didn't really have a plan, to be honest. I just knew I wanted to stay in London for the time being and bought."

He nodded and obeyed the navigation by hooking a left, heading toward Vauxhall Bridge.

"What do you do?" Jasmine asked me.

"I run a vlog," I told her.

"What kind?" she asked.

"Hair, makeup, fashion. I started off reviewing products, and my audience grew. As they grew, so did my range. I adapt as I go."

"Interesting," she said.

"She works with FACE London," Oliver added, shocking me. "Have you not seen their new campaign? She's their new face."

"Where would I have seen it?" Jasmine asked,

sounding bored.

"Sides of buses, maybe? She's got a billboard in Oxford Square," he answered.

"You do?" Jasmine asked, perking up a bit.

"Uh, yeah, it's just for fashion week, though."

Oh my God, Oliver's seen *me!*

"Well, good on you," Jasmine offered cordially, turning around. Her facial expression wasn't as generous as her message. It made her look ugly somehow and brought her down closer to my level.

Jasmine began to face the front again but her eyes shot wide when she saw my bag setting on the seat next to me. "Is that a *Zoe* bag?" she asked, not bothering to hide her disbelief.

"Uh, yeah," I answered, not sure what else to say.

Jasmine whipped her head toward Oliver. "You said your queue was too long, that I had to wait like the rest, that it wouldn't be right otherwise, but you made one for *her*?"

"*Jasmine,*" Oliver tried to soothe. It was the wrong thing to say. I knew it, but he didn't.

"What the hell, Oliver?" Jasmine shouted. Bingo. "What exactly is this girl to you?"

I sank into my seat.

"She's Graham's ex-girlfriend," he explained, which meant she'd met Graham. I caught his eyes in the rearview. "She helped me market the bag, instructed me how to get it out here. It worked. I was repaying her the favor by giving her the original."

"The original!" Jasmine yelled. "You told me that one was off limits even to your *girlfriend.*"

Girlfriend! Oh my God. What a cluster.

While I debated on whether or not to say anything, Oliver said, "It was. It was meant for her. It was a gift for her long before I met you."

I knew what he meant by that. He was referring to the fact that he'd tried to give it to me, but I'd refused, but *Jasmine* took that in an entirely different way.

"Let me out of the car," she insisted, grasping her door handle.

"Wait, wait!" I called out. I made a move to touch her shoulder but thought better of it. "I promise this doesn't mean anything! He gave it to me once and I was too uncomfortable to take it. I really did help him with the release."

Jasmine sat back and looked at me. "Did you date?" she asked.

"No," I insisted. Not a total lie.

"Oliver?" Jasmine asked.

"We were friends. Now we are merely acquaintances," he explained.

Jasmine calmed but the statement wounded me, deflated me.

"*You have arrived at your destination*," the navigation system announced.

I scrambled for the door and threw it open. "Thank you for the ride. Please, go on ahead to Preston's. No need to wait. I'll catch a taxi."

I ran up to the main door of the converted house my flat was in. I stuck in my key. I turned to wave but they both sat there staring at me. I remembered my torn outfit and turned beet red. I laid my bag against the tear and turned the key.

Oliver looked from Jasmine to me then back at

Jasmine then pulled away. I knocked on Claire's door. When she answered, I turned around to show her what happened.

"Bloody hell!"

"I know," I whined.

"Come on then," she said, dragging me by my hand up to my flat.

My eyes teared up. "He was there, Claire."

Claire stopped on her step briefly before continuing. "Did he see this little fiasco?" she asked, gesturing with a finger.

"Front and center."

"Well, at least your ass looks fabulous."

I burst out laughing and the tears came with it. "He had a girl with him, his girlfriend, actually."

This time Claire looked at me. "I thought you said he didn't do monogamy."

"He doesn't—didn't."

"Okay, well, how long?"

"I don't know." I sighed. "She's very pretty and seems nice enough."

"That puts a damper on things, doesn't it?" she stated as I stuck my key into my door and let us both in.

"Yes." I sniffed.

"Are you going to the luncheon?" she asked.

I set Oliver's bag on the table and stared at it while I answered. "If I wasn't representing FACE, I'd be in my bed right now eating Ben & Jerry's Cherry Garcia."

"Oh, Penelope, that bad? I'm sorry," she said, rounding the table to see me.

"It was pretty humiliating." I tried to smile but it didn't work. "I have to find something else to wear and try to book it to the luncheon."

"Are you sure you can't slip out of it?"

I nodded. "I have to go. I'm sure they would understand, but I don't shirk my responsibilities. Besides, it's my livelihood. Just have to suck it up, buttercup."

Claire sighed. "Right, then let's get you changed."

I threw on my leather leggings, a pair of clunky heels, and an off-shoulder sweater. Henry had pinned part of my hair up earlier and I removed the pins, letting my hair fall down naturally. I touched up my eye makeup thanks to my little crying session as well as my lipstick.

"How's that?" I asked.

"Not so shabby for last minute," she told me.

"You sure?"

"It's fine, Pen. You're going to knock their socks off when you arrive *fashionably* late."

I ran down and was greeted by a cabbie whom Claire had signaled for from the window. I told him I'd give him an extra tenner if he stepped on it. He got me there in lightning-quick time. I stepped out of the cab and into the Preston's lobby.

"I'm sorry, this is a private event," the hostess said.

"Oh, yes, sorry," I said, bringing out my invite and handing it over. "I'm a tad late."

She took the invite. "You're fine," she said. "They've only started seating everyone. No one will even notice."

I sighed. "Oh, thank God."

She smiled and opened the door for me. I slipped in and noticed a few mingling groups of people talking who had yet to sit. Oliver and Jasmine sat at a table near the podium, their bodies turned into one another. Frantic for them not to notice me, I spotted a table at the very, very back with three empty chairs.

"So sorry," I told a guy about my age, I guessed, sitting alone, "but are any of these taken?"

"No," he said with an American accent. "Here," he said, standing up and pulling my chair out for me.

"Thank you," I told him as I sat.

"Thank God you're American. Conversation has been a little lacking for me. My last seat mate was German. After my thousandth 'excuse me?' he decided to excuse himself instead."

I laughed.

"Where are you from?" I asked.

"Los Angeles. You?"

"I'm from Dallas, but I've lived here for over a year." *Could that be true? Have I been here this long?*

"That's cool. What do you do that warrants such a prestigious invite?" he sarcastically bit out, signaling around us with an exaggerated hand.

I giggled. "I run a vlog."

"Have I heard of you?"

"Depends," I kidded. Men usually had no idea who I was.

"What's your name?" he asked.

"Penelope Beckett."

"I actually know you," he said.

"No, you don't. Shut up!" I laughed.

"I do," he insisted. "I really do."

"Fine. Prove it." He brought up an app on his phone that showed one of my videos. "Oh my gosh, you do know who I am." I looked at the site he pulled up and laughed again. "Does a joke video site count, though?"

His ears turned red. "It does if they tag the video with

'viral hot chick.'"

I rolled my eyes. "And what, pray tell, warrants your presence here?"

"I am but a lowly photojournalist, so low on the totem pole they stuck me out here to cover the smaller events."

"For what publication?" I asked.

"I'd rather not say."

"Why's that?"

"Because if I can't answer that question with *TIME* magazine, then what's the point?"

I nodded. "I can respect that."

"Can I?" he asked, holding up his camera.

"Oh my gosh, I guess. It's pointless because no one knows who I am, though."

"If it's all the same, I'd appreciate it. If I don't give them something to work with, they'll get pissed and will fire me."

"Well, if it'll put food in your belly," I teased.

I smiled and tilted my head for him. He took the shot and looked down at his camera.

"What was your name?"

He stuck out his hand. "Jasper Turner, at your service."

I shook it. "Nice to meet you, Jasper."

"Excuse me, ladies and gentlemen," a woman at the podium announced through a microphone.

"Will the owner of an eighty-seven Buick LeSabre please approach the podium? You've left your lights on," I mocked under my breath.

"Eighty-seven was a banner year for the LeSabre," Jasper pitched in.

"These people have probably never even seen a

LeSabre." I giggled.

"Probably not an eighty-seven, but I think they were here twenty years before that."

"Get out of town. How do you know that?"

"I'm a guy."

"So what?"

"What color bra should you were with a black dress?" he asked.

"Oh, nude for sure," I answered without hesitation.

"See?" he asked, shrugging.

"Yes, actually, I do." I giggled.

The woman had gone on and on about the integral importance of modern-day fashion on the world. It was tedious to listen to.

"I mean, I love fashion," I said, "but it's not quite the difference between life or *death*."

"To them, it is."

"Priorities. Get 'em."

"No kidding," he said then smiled. "You feel like getting a drink after this?"

I didn't know what to say. I mean, I wasn't dating anyone. I wasn't tied to anyone. Graham was long over with and Oliver, well, Oli was very much taken. I had no reason not to. He was a cute, funny boy and he was interested. He seemed like zero drama. I opened my mouth to speak but nothing came out.

"Listen," he said, "I didn't mean to put you on the spot or anything..."

"No!" I said. "I'd like to. Seriously, it was only unexpected. It's been *a while*," I breathed.

"Okay, well, then what do you say?"

"Uh, yeah, of course. I have to go to that industry

thing at seven. Are you going?" I asked.

"No journalists allowed."

"Really?"

"Yeah, they check your bags for cameras. Plus, you have to be invited." He smiled.

"I can bring a date. Would you like to come with me? Leave the camera at home and let your hair down."

He playfully untucked his chin-length hair from behind his ear. "Done."

We talked our way through lunch and two more speakers, which was terrible. Both Jasper and I got all the pictures we needed or hoped to get. He got a few of the more serious images during the speeches, which would mean nothing to my viewers so I let those shots go and focused on the candid shots of celebrity. Jasper was easy to talk to, good looking, funny. There's a but in there, as you know. I won't say it, though.

Chapter Eighteen

The club blasted music so loud you could hear it from the sidewalk a block down. I had no idea how I was going to be able to get to know Jasper under noise like that, but I supposed we'd figure it out. We'd exchanged numbers before we left the luncheon, so I texted him letting him know to meet me across the street from the club. He texted back he'd arrive in ten minutes.

I never carried a purse or clutch on the very rare occasions I frequented clubs because it was more a liability than a help. Instead, I tucked my ID, cash, and a lipstick in the crevices of my bra. It wasn't the classiest move, I admit, but I didn't necessarily care.

I adjusted my bracelets on my arm as I waited. I'd recorded a vlog before I left, part of a segment I called "Get Ready With Me." Not exactly the cleverest of titles, but it did the trick, and it was pretty popular. I straightened my hair pin straight and it fell at my waist. Whenever I curled it for warm outings, it always fell and looked terrible. I wore black hose, black shorts, and clunky combats. I never wore skirts to clubs, too many creepers. Nor did I wear heels in a crowded place like a club because they were hard enough to navigate without a hundred bodies trampling on your toes. I chose a white bandage-waist crop top where the bandage that wrapped my waist was black as well as the throat collar hem. Only a sliver of my waist showed. Didn't want to give too much of the goods away. As I'd told my viewers, clubwear has to have an edge of practicality to it. Anything a boy could secretly lift or reach under was off limits. This was the world we lived in, after all. I drowned my arms in silver bracelets with geometric patterns throughout. My makeup was much darker than it had been in the day. I went for a smokey-eye look and bright red lipstick.

After ten minutes, I was starting to think I'd changed the way I looked so dramatically that Jasper wouldn't recognize me.

"Penelope!" I heard behind me.

I smiled and turned around only to find *Oliver*. My smile fell and I gulped. Oliver and *Jasmine*. She didn't follow any of my club attire rules. Short skirt. Again. Short top. That was new. Ridiculously high heels. I had to peer up into her eyes.

"Oh, hey!" I said in an attempt to sound cheery and not at all the insecure, intimidated nincompoop I really was.

"What are you doing out here?" Oliver asked.

"Just waiting for my date," I explained, looking around for Jasper. I didn't see him.

Jasmine's shoulders relaxed.

Oliver looked surprised. "Your *date*?"

I rolled my eyes. "Yes, my *date*."

"Who is he?" he asked.

"A photojournalist I met today at the luncheon. Jasper something," I said, snapping my fingers over and over, trying to remember his last name. I pointed at the sky. "Turner! Jasper Turner."

"My ears are burning!" I heard someone shout with an exaggerated laugh.

I glanced over my shoulder at one very adorable-looking Jasper Turner. He wasn't as tall as Oliver, didn't have that well-kept *Gentlemen's Quarterly* thing happening that Oliver had, but he was very sweet looking with his disheveled button-up shirt with rolled-up sleeves, black jeans, and Chuck Taylors. His caramel hair was mussed and tucked behind his ears. His smile was so big it made my heart stutter a little. *That's a good sign.*

"Hey! You made it!"

"In the flesh." He extended a fist and I bumped one with his. "It's good to see you," he said, his cheeks turning a little pink. He was a charmer, that was for sure, and he didn't even try.

I grabbed his arm and brought him in front of Oliver and Jasmine. "Jasper this is Oliver Finn and his girlfriend, Jasmine."

"Hello, mate," Oliver greeted, sticking out his hand to shake Jasper's.

Jasper grasped it. "Nice to meet you," he said, then dropped his hand to extend it toward Jasmine. "Nice to meet you as well," he said as she took it.

He tucked both hands into the pockets of his jeans. "Are you going to this party?" he asked them, throwing his head in the direction of the club.

"We are," Oliver replied, his expression passive and,

frankly, confusing.

"Shall we?" Jasper asked, removing his left hand and holding it out for me.

I slid my palm into his. It felt nice there, his fingers fit perfectly with mine. He hit the crosswalk button at the corner and led me across the street. Oli and Jasmine followed just behind, the heat of Oliver's stare was palpable. My free hand went to the back of my neck.

At the door I yelled my name to the gatekeeper and he checked it off the list then let us inside. I didn't know if I should wait for Oliver. It was a little weird, our situation, something I hadn't anticipated, and didn't know the protocol. Jasper solved my dilemma for me by speaking into my ear.

"Let's hit the bar first!"

I nodded and we tucked in between two people waiting for the bartender's attention. Jasper didn't let go of my hand. "What'll you have?" he asked.

"A Guinness, please?"

Jasper looked shocked. "Guinness!"

I nodded, used to this reaction. "I hate light beers!" I explained.

"I like a stout drinker." He winked.

It was a few minutes of waiting, but eventually he ordered two pints of Guinness, and we escaped the crowd surrounding the bar, laughing when a woman elbowed herself into our old place.

Jasper took a sip from his beer. "So what made you move to London?" he shouted over the din of the music.

How to answer this? "I met a guy last year in Dallas, we fell in love quickly, and he convinced me to move home with him. I can work from anywhere, as you know, and thought it would be fun."

"But it didn't work out?"

I laughed. "Uh, no, it most definitely did not work out."

"I'd say I was sorry but I'm not." He smiled.

I smiled back, not sure how I felt about his comment. "When do you head back?" I asked.

"Five days."

I bit my bottom lip. "Are you having fun in the LDN?"

"I am now," he flirted.

"You're good," I told him.

He jokingly dusted his shoulder. "I try."

"It's nice to run into an American," I admitted.

"Oh yeah?" He laughed. "Why's that?"

"Londoners don't mean anything they say!" Jasper's shoulders shook with laughter. "It's hard to get a straight answer out of anyone. American boys will just come out and tell you. 'I dig you, let's have a drink.' London boys hem and haw, lead you on for weeks. It's very bad for the self-esteem."

"That's hilarious."

"They're still some of my favorite people, though, and they dress better than we do."

"That I will agree to," he said, pulling at the hem of his wrinkled shirt and staring at the others around us.

I giggled. "You look really cute, Jasper."

The tips of his ears turned red and his hand went to the back of his neck. "Thanks," he said. He looked at me and swallowed. "You look really beautiful, Penelope."

"Thanks, Jasper."

"How old are you?" he asked.

"Twenty-two. I'll be twenty-three in three days,

though."

"Get the hell out! We should do something fun."

"That sounds cool," I said, not really sure if I wanted to spend my birthday with someone I barely knew. "How old are you?" I asked him.

"Twenty-four."

"A very good age, I think. It suits you."

Jasper shrugged. "It isn't anything like I thought it would be."

"Why?"

"You remember when you were a kid and you thought the phrase 'When I grow up' at least a hundred times a day?"

"Of course."

"Well, I think being a grown-up sucks."

"Not going to argue with you there."

"It's, like, we're old enough to pay our own way, but that pay usually bites. We don't get to do any of the things we really want to do because we're always broke. Plus, I still feel like I need to talk to my mom every day. I still need that security." He blushed. "Is that pathetic?"

"Uh, no, not at freaking all. I still write my mom every day. I have to or I feel really alone or—or *something*. It's hard to explain."

"You don't have to 'cause I get it."

"Maybe we're just sheltered?" I asked.

Jasper laughed. "That's very possible. In my case, more than possible." He cleared his throat. "So, Dallas, do you want to dance with LA?"

"Can you rumba?"

He looked stricken. "Not at all."

"Good," I teased, "neither can I." He bumped his

shoulder into mine.

We set our empty glasses on a nearby table. He grabbed my hand and led me out onto the dance floor. We jumped around, laughing like idiots, not really caring about the people around us, and singing the lyrics of the songs to one another. He was a surprisingly good dancer and we found a rhythm between us that worked well.

After three or four songs, we left to get some water, then hit the dance floor again. Eventually they played a slow song and Jasper grabbed my hands, placing them behind his neck, then put his fingers on my hips.

"Very ninth grade," he teased.

"Well, Jason Mraz isn't playing and I don't have a face full of metal so, nothing like ninth."

"There you are!" a voice yelled from behind us. We both turned to spot Oli. "We've got a VIP room. You should join us!"

Jasper looked at me and shrugged. "It'd be nice to sit, right?"

Oliver stared at me, a knowing smirk on his face. If I said no, Jasper would want to know why. I could lie, but that wasn't my MO. If I said yes, though, Oliver would be able to watch us. Either way he would win. "Um, yeah, sure."

Jasper grasped my hand and we followed Oliver. His body swayed with every long stride. He reminded me of an animal slinking through tall grass, and I couldn't help imagining myself as his prey. "When I die, I want to come back as him. He's freakin' cool!" Jasper said, startling me back to the present. *That doesn't help*, I thought.

Oliver ascended the short staircase, holding back the heavy curtain that hid the raised room that looked over the dance floor. When Oliver let the curtain drop, the obnoxious music dialed down a few notches. Jasper and I looked at one another and sighed with relief then laughed. Oliver's brows pinched.

There were at least ten people elegantly draped across a moon-shaped couch. They all acted put out when Jasper and I squeezed in two couples down from Oliver and Jasmine. We were jammed so closely together I could smell Jasper's cologne.

"Feel a little bit better?" he asked me.

"I really do." I giggled. "I'm not a big fan of clubs," I admitted.

"Note to self," he said, tapping his temple. "So what do you like?"

"I like going out but usually places that don't charge ten pounds for one drink. I like more intimate places, pubs-off-the-beaten-path kind of thing."

He nodded.

"What are you both on about then?" Oliver asked, leaning forward.

Everyone turned to look at us. "Oh, I was just trying to glean ideas from Penelope on what she'd like to do for her birthday," Jasper explained.

Oliver smiled. "That's right. You're twenty-three this Friday." Oliver sat back casually, throwing his arms over the back of the sofa. "You know, I could throw you a party, if you like? Bring you 'round the house again?"

The offer knocked the wind out of me. "Oh, I couldn't impose," I sputtered.

As I said this, Jasmine scooted forward, her hand landing on Oliver's knee, and nervously giggled. "Oliver, she won't want that!"

Oliver ignored them and spoke only to me. "No, no. I *insist.*"

Chapter
Nineteen

Jasper worked most of the days leading up to my birthday. We enjoyed a text friendship and one dinner together. We laughed a lot. Turns out, the chemistry just wasn't really there for either of us, but we agreed we would be great friends and promised to stay that way.

I'd explained to him in great detail at the dinner the predicament between Oliver and me.

"He made this sort of," I said, gesturing wildly with my hands, "declaration to me."

Jasper leaned forward, a look of wonder on his face. "Wow," he whispered. "What did you say?"

"I'd just gotten my heart stomped on by Graham. I wasn't in a place to *hear* him, if you know what I mean? B-but if it had been any other time, any other day, I think the message would have come across loud and clear and with real meaning."

"Wow," Jasper said again.

"And he wasn't into monogamy. I mean *really* wasn't into it."

He looked confused. "But he has that girlfriend. The blonde. What's her name?"

"Jasmine. And I know! What the hell? Last time I was around him, it was a different girl every week," I said, snapping my fingers. "Now he's Mr. Boyfriend?"

Jasper sat back in his chair and folded his arms across his chest. "I have him pegged. He's trying on a relationship, seeing how it feels, seeing if he likes it."

I was appalled. "Surely not. That's a despicable thing to do to someone. I don't think Oliver would do that."

"I didn't say he didn't dig Jasmine. I'm just saying he's testing relationship waters."

I can't believe I'm admitting to this, but I thought I liked it better when I thought he was using Jasmine. "Oh."

Our food arrived and we dug in.

"Are you going to come to my birthday party?" I asked him.

He took a bite. "Yeah, man, of course."

"Cool beans."

"Yeah, peachy keen," he teased.

"Shut up."

"No, you shut up."

"No, you shut up."

Jasper and I looked at one another for a brief moment before bursting into laughter.

We didn't stay long after that. He kissed my cheek on our way out and told me he'd see me the next day at the party. Oliver had sent evites to everyone, including myself, but failed to send one to Jasper. To be fair, Oliver hadn't known Jasper's email, but he could have asked.

As I walked toward the tube, my phone rang. Oliver. *Holy cannoli.*

I shifted the button to answer. "Hello?"

"Hello, Pen, it's Oli."

"Hey, man. What's up?"

"Uh, I was just at the store to get a few things for tomorrow night and I thought you might want to have a say and all that since it's your big day and all."

I felt my face flush. "Um, well, okay," I replied.

"Are you busy?" he asked.

"Well, um, no, not now," I answered.

"Not on some hot date with Jasper tonight then?" he teased.

"I just left dinner with him, actually," I bit back. *Don't fish if you don't want what you catch, sucker.*

"Oh, right then." He cleared his throat. "I'm at that party store on Acton. Do you mind meeting up?"

"Not at all," I lied. "I'm only about ten minutes away. I-is Jasmine with you?"

"No." He paused. "I, well, we're no longer seeing one another."

I sucked in a breath and hoped he didn't hear it. "Oh goodness, I'm sorry."

"It's okay. It's ... we decided to go our separate ways."

I took a deep breath. "I hope it was nothing I did."

"No!" he insisted. "She had a desire to see other people. We'd only just tried to be exclusive and last night she admitted she'd already agreed to go out with another guy."

I winced. "Jeez, Oli, that sucks."

He sighed deeply. "It's fine, Pen." Another pause. "See you in ten?" he asked.

"See you," I said and hung up.

My heart was in my throat as I laid my card on the

Oyster pod on the turnstile and caught the train toward Acton. I found the store fairly easily but didn't go directly in. I was too keyed up, too afraid of what could be said or wouldn't be said. I was no longer protected by the buffer that was Jasmine. A girl who'd just, for lack of a better word, dumped him.

I opened the door and a little bell overhead chimed, announcing my presence.

"How's it!" the lady at the counter cooed.

"Evening," I greeted, my pulse speeding up at the prospect of seeing Oliver soon. I turned my head side to side looking for him.

"If you're looking for that tall chap," she said, pointing to the back corner of the store. "He's just back there with my assistant."

"Thank you," I told her, hiking my Zoe farther up my arm.

I rounded an aisle only to come across a rotund woman in her fifties leaning into Oliver a little too closely and purring something into his ear. When his desperate eyes met mine, I fought a smile.

"Darling!" he shouted a little too loudly, prying the woman off his arm. "There you are!"

He sidled up to me. "Just go with it," he whispered, embracing me, sending shivers down my spine.

His wide eyes met mine so I nodded.

"Lover!" I laid on thickly. Throwing my arms around his neck, I threaded my fingers through his hair. "I've missed you so! Don't ever leave my side again. Promise me," I pleaded, clutching my body to his. Oliver snorted and shook his head. I pulled away, grasping his shoulders, fixing a manic expression on my face. "If I have to go even a minute more without your hand in mine, I'll die. *Die!*"

"You're overselling it," he gritted out between his teeth.

Me? I mouthed.

He bit back a smile as the lady passed us grumbling, "Call if you need anything."

I let go of him and doubled over in a silent laugh.

He kept shaking his head. "You are incorrigible, Penelope Beckett."

"At your service," I said, standing upright and saluting him.

He glanced at me, making my insides flip-flop. He turned his gaze from mine and studied the ceiling.

"In all seriousness, though," I said, stealing back his attention, "are you okay?"

"Yeah, why wouldn't I be?" he asked, a confused expression on his face.

"Because of your breakup?"

"Oh yeah. Yeah, I'm fine."

"I'm still sorry," I told him.

"It's okay, Pen, really," he said, refusing to look at my face. He grabbed my hand, pouring butterflies into my belly, and led me to an aisle full of themed decorations.

"So many to choose from," he said, dropping my hand and extending his arms.

He picked up a large straw sombrero and placed it on my head.

"*Muy caliente*," he teased, then took it off and put it back on its shelf. "Do you have any more shows tomorrow?" he asked.

"None," I told him, picking up maracas and giving them a good shake.

"I have a show mid-morning tomorrow. Alice & Emma? Heard of them?"

"Of course," I said, perusing the party decorations.

Oliver lifted a pack of party plates that read *Hip Cat* across them. He studied them closely. "I, uh," he said then cleared his throat, "I have an extra ticket if you'd like to go with me."

He laid down the pack of plates and tucked a hand into the front pocket of his jeans as he looked at me, waiting for my answer. It gave me butterflies.

My heart raced and I swallowed hard. "Yeah, I think that would be cool. What time?"

"Ten a.m. Should I pick you up?"

"That's fine. Might be easier to take a cab, though? I think it's a pretty popular show, be a nightmare to find parking."

His shoulders slumped a little. He looked deflated. "Right, yeah, of course."

"How about we meet up for breakfast beforehand then we can hitch it together to the show?"

He perked up, which gave me such a rush to see him physically react to me like that. "That'd be great." He smiled. "Where should we go?"

"Your choice," I said, looking toward the shelves again. If I'd looked at him anymore, I felt like my heart would explode. I fingered a few plastic crowns.

"Okay, how about Regency?" he asked.

I bit my lip and begged my heart to slow down. Regency was the little café where Graham and all his mates, including Oliver, would meet on Saturday mornings after Friday-night bashes. It brought forth bittersweet memories for me.

"Yeah, of course. Love that place," I told him. It was a half-truth.

"Right, then that's settled. Come now, love, help me grab a few things for tomorrow."

We grabbed a bunch of luau stuff and went to the counter.

As the woman who greeted me when I entered the store rang up everything, Oli leaned on the counter, facing me.

"I like the bag on you, Pen."

"Do you?" I asked.

"It suits you."

"Thank you."

He studied me for a moment. "What are you doing for the rest of the evening?" he asked.

"Why do you ask?"

"Because I'd like to talk to you."

My heart jumped into my throat. "What about?"

He didn't answer my question. Instead he said, "I'm happy you're in London." He stood and brought himself inches from my face. "Penelope?" he asked.

"Yes?" I whispered.

"Are you dating that American bloke?"

"J-Jasper?" I stuttered when I took in Oliver's face. His hair had fallen forward slightly and hung over his right eye.

"Yes, that one," he replied, dismissing Jasper with the statement, letting me know what he really thought of him.

My throat went dry. "No, um, we decided we'd be better off friends."

A slow smile spread across his mouth, making him

look a little dangerous. "That's too bad," he told me, his tone implying just the opposite and making my blood run hot in my veins.

The cashier must have spoken, but I didn't hear her, too engrossed in Oliver's expression and his warming proximity. Without breaking his stare, Oliver produced a card and handed it over. Only after the woman ran the card and handed it back did he break his gaze, leaving me dazed and confused where I stood.

He grabbed the bags as well as my hand, leading me toward the store exit.

"I could cook an egg on this counter now with the heat comin' off you two," the cashier teased then laughed.

We stopped on the sidewalk outside the store. He peered down at me and without skipping a beat, asked, "How *do* you like your eggs, Penelope Beckett?"

My mouth gaped open. "I—" I began, but he interrupted.

"Never mind that," he stated, reaching into his pocket and studying the building across the street. "I believe I remember now. Eggs Benedict."

"That's right," I told him, feeling a little starstruck.

"Isn't that ironic?" he said, pulling a tin from his pocket.

"How so?"

He offered me a wintergreen mint and I took it before he took one for himself then pocketed the tin once more. He placed the mint on his tongue and I was utterly distracted by his mouth.

"Benedict Arnold was an American traitor?"

My tongue tingled, felt heavy. "Yes," I confirmed.

He leaned in close and I had to crane my neck to see

into his eyes. "Enticed by the lure of a Brit, was he not?"

He winded me, stole the breaths right out of me. I panted and nodded, unable to answer.

He gamely smiled at the passing cars. "Interesting." I stood next to him, astounded. "Come, Pen," he said, taking my hand again and leading me down the street. "Let's have a bit of fun. What say you?"

"Uh-huh," I dumbly replied.

We walked a block to his car and he threw his bags into the backseat, never letting go of my hand, then opened the passenger door for me. I climbed in and he closed the door before scaling the front of the car, settling into the driver's side. My eyes never left him. He was like a different species of animal, too silver-tongued, too facile to be human.

"Since you've had dinner, how about a drink?" he asked.

"A drink would be fine," I managed to spit out despite the fact he'd rendered me dumbstruck.

"I know just the place," he promised, starting the car and jetting out into the street.

We whipped throughout his London neighborhood and landed at a rather cozy-looking pub called The Red Undertaker. Oliver parked and opened my door for me, taking my hand yet again, and locking the car. He opened the bright red door to the pub for me and it was as I suspected, incredibly intimate. A long, galley-like configuration. The long bar ran half the length of the room with long tables and benches lining the opposite side with barely enough room to walk down the center walkway. Just at the center of the room, opposite the bar, and breaking up the line of tables, was a marble fireplace with a small fire and small love seat facing that. *Intimate*, was all I could think. And it was vacant.

Oliver led me to the seat, took my jacket from me, and laid it across one arm along with his. "I'll just check these," he said, escaping toward the back coat check.

I watched him retreat and my heart beat into my throat. "Oh my God," I whispered to no one.

My hands shook at my sides as I stared at the fire.

"Buy you a drink, love?" a kept-looking young guy asked.

I turned my body better toward him. "That's kind, thank you, but I'm with someone," I told him.

Oh my God, am I here with *Oliver? Is this really happening?*

"No problem," he said with a wave and walked away.

"Checked," a voice to my left told me.

I cut my head toward Oliver then turned the rest of my body. He nestled himself beside me comfortably, confidently, and unbuttoned his shirt cuffs. He studied me as he did this and I felt my skin burn to impossible temperatures. He began to roll one sleeve up a defined forearm and my eyes swung to the movement.

I leaned forward. "Let me," I told him, taking the sleeve in my hands.

With each revolution, my shaking fingers grazed his broiling skin and my stomach plummeted to my feet. He watched me with hooded eyes, his mouth slightly parted. When I reached just under his elbow, my hands lingered a moment before falling away. Without a word, he offered the other arm. Biting my bottom lip, I reached out and rolled the other sleeve, taking my time with it, knowing he had no more sleeves to roll, no more skin to know. I looked into his smoldering expression. I was at an impasse. If I continued to touch him anymore, there'd be no such pretense. And he knew it.

A waitress brought two tumblers of an amber-colored liquid and offered them to us. I took one and Oliver took the other. She walked away toward the bar again.

"What is this?" I asked.

"Guess."

"Glenlivet," I told him without even taking a sip.

"You would be correct."

I took a deep, shaky breath, remembering the night we'd shared Glenlivet. This night had a completely different tone to it, and I thought he wanted me to know that. I thought he was rebadging that whisky between us. It worked.

I studied my fingers for a moment before meeting his gaze. He sat there with me, looking assured, his right arm draped across the back of the seat. His hand gripped the back edge of our sofa, his knuckles white with the effort. Those bloodless fingers told me of the war brewing within his cool exterior, and that knowledge did things to my insides.

He brought the glass to his lips and downed the liquid in its entirety, letting the empty glass rest on his left knee, his long fingers braced around the tumbler.

"Talk," he ordered after I took a nervous swig.

"What do you want me to say?"

"If you've been in London all this time," his deep voice crooned, "why not come see me?"

I swallowed hard and stared into the fire. "I don't know."

He barked a short laugh. "Yes, you do."

I took another sip and let the liquid warm me up from the inside. I set the tumbler on the small section of seat between us, keeping my fingers around its rim, and leaned forward. "I'm afraid of you, Oliver Finn."

Oliver stopped breathing. I saw it. His chest settled still and he sat upright, leaning toward me, his face inches from mine.

"I won't argue with that," he revealed.

"Why?" I asked.

"Because you should be afraid of me."

"I am, but my reasons are my own. I wonder, though, what yours are," I whispered.

He gave me that same smile again, the one that revealed he knew much, but would divulge none of it.

"Keep your secrets then," I told him, downing the remaining contents of my drink and sitting back up.

Oliver took my empty glass from me, his fingers grazing mine, sending tingles down my legs. He held up his along with mine as the waitress passed and ordered two more. The liquid courage was a successful endeavor.

"Still hold no belief in regrets?" he asked me when she returned with our second round, handing over a glass.

Feeling bold, I took both in my hands and set them at the small table at our feet. Looking for an excuse to touch him, I ignored his question and reached for his fitted vest, pulling him toward me. He let me, his eyes targeted on my lips. I untucked his tie, pulling it out slowly, then undid the knot, dragging the length from around his neck, walking my hands up the fabric as I drew it down. He closed his eyes briefly and swallowed. I followed the line of his throat as he did this and smiled. He opened his eyes and stared at me. I made a show of wrapping the tie slowly around my hand. My fingers went to his neck and undid his collar button, peeling it back, and exposing his throat.

When I had no more to touch without it looking too brazen, I sat back. He stared at me and a lazy, knowing smile grew, which made the butterflies in my stomach dive and climb. I felt my cheeks flush but kept his gaze while I pulled at the end of the tie around my hand, letting it unravel, the movement swishing the fabric against my skin, sending chills up my arm. I held it up and let it coil in the seat between us.

He swallowed. "That was…"

"Interesting?" I bantered, stealing his word from outside the shop earlier.

He nodded.

If I'm doing this, I thought, pressing my body against his. I brought my lips to his ear.

"I'm no traitor," I whispered.

I felt his shoulders shake with laughter as I smiled into his neck.

He turned and spoke his words against the skin of my throat. "You'll defect. I can be very persuasive."

I shifted my head slowly from side to side, letting the ends of my hair sway across his arms. "Would you settle for dual citizenship?" I flirted.

"No," he taunted, the fingers of his right hand finding the wrist of my left. He wrapped them around and his thumb found my pulse point, pressing lightly. "I'll have not but a full allegiance," he demanded.

He dipped his head and I gasped softly as his lips found my collarbone. "Pen," he said, running his teeth along the bone.

"Hmm?"

"You're much better at this than I could have possibly imagined," he admitted.

He pulled back, waiting for a response. I suppose he wanted to see my face when I answered. I lightly shrugged one shoulder instead, making him laugh.

"Should we go back to my place?" he asked.

Now it was my turn to smile. I reached out with my right hand and ran my fingers through the top of his hair. His head fell back somewhat before falling forward when I brought my fingers down the back of his neck then around to rest on his shoulder. He stared at me, waiting.

"No, there'll be none of that, sir," I answered.

His eyes formed slits and a devilish smile reached across his incredible mouth. "Oh, Pen, I believe you're the most fun I've ever had."

"I guarantee it."

"Do you now?" he flirted, resting both his hands along my jawline.

He let both slide down the sides of my neck, bringing his right hand around, letting his fingers settle softly around my throat. He leaned in and kissed once below my left ear, rounding halfway along my jaw before pushing my head back, exposing the side of my throat. My breaths sped then, despite my desperate attempt to control them, and I felt a deep, rumbling laugh vibrate against the skin there all the way into my chest. He had me, he was certain of it.

With the added confidence that came with this new conviction, he kept his face buried in my throat but let his hands fall to my waist, gripping there and yanking me closer. An involuntary gasp followed and his fingers applied even more pressure.

"Pen," his voice thundered across my skin. "I want to kiss you."

"*Oh my God*," I whispered.

"But it won't be here," he explained while dragging his lips up my throat.

"Why not?"

"Because I'll be damned if the first time I get to taste you is in a public house." He sat up, his eyes looking a little intoxicated by the moment. I wondered if mine matched. I was sure they did. "Come to my house."

"No."

He smiled. "I'll touch your lips with mine only." He crossed his heart with his thumb. "On my honor. After, you can stay in your old room, or I'll take you home. Your choice."

I considered him. "Just a kiss?"

"A single kiss, madam, I assure you."

"What time is it?" I asked.

"Ten."

"Take me to your place, Oliver Finn."

He shot up like a rocket. "Stay," he ordered, a wild look in his eyes. "Whatever you do, do not change your mind."

He looked to his right and nodded at the bartender, signaling he wanted his check. He ran his hands through his hair, straightening out the lovely mess I'd created, which secretly disappointed me because that territory had been marked—and it was mine. He walked with purpose toward the coat check. Returning with our coats, I watched his lean, muscled body hover over the bar top, reaching for a pen and signing the tab to close it. He shook hands with the bartenders and turned toward me.

My left hand found the back of the love seat's edge as I watched him stalk toward me, my breaths speeding up with every step he took my direction. He terrified *and* excited me, and I decided in that moment that was the best combination of sensations I'd ever felt. He was the only one I'd met who had ever produced them. I stood, clutching my bag to my body, and waited for him to come to me.

"Miss Beckett," he greeted when he reached me.

"Mr. Finn."

He laid his jacket over the back of the love seat and held my own out for me as I slipped my arms through. Stepping closer, he closed the jacket, buttoning me up from the top to the bottom. He smiled at me as he did it.

"It's only fair," he taunted.

When he was done, he picked up his own, not bothering to put it on, then held out his hand. I placed a palm over his and he laced his fingers with mine. Practically sprinting out of the pub, he pulled me behind him to his car, throwing open the passenger side door and placing me inside. Within two minutes we were at his house, pulling into his garage.

Memories of that last day flooded me but before I had time to process them, Oliver had removed me from the car, picking me up and jogging with me up the stairs.

"No casts this time," he said with a wink.

Bolting through the door, he set me on my feet.

He smiled, though I could barely see it in the dark of the room, our only light from the lamps outside.

"Welcome back," he said.

I returned the smile.

"I want to tell you so many things," he revealed to the floor, his hands clasped behind his back, "but I'm not sure where to begin." He shifted his head even closer. "I-I'll start with the easy things." His dazzling eyes found mine and he smiled. "It's so effortless to be with you, Pen. The mere act of holding your hand thrills me in ways you couldn't possibly comprehend. Hearing your voice is a balm to my soul. Feeling your skin, looking into your eyes, knowing your touch is a heaven I will never grow accustomed to. I am utterly enchanted by you and that affection, that fever, has not once wavered, not in the year I've known you, not once. I've tried time and time again to distract myself from you, tried to come to terms with it, and I'm worn out from trying. It's exhausting. I want you, Penelope. I can count the things I am desperate for on one hand, on a single finger. You. I want *you*. Only you."

I wanted him to kiss me, to fulfill his promise in the pub, yet he stood stock-still, refusing to close the gap between us. It was up to me. He was telling me it was up to me.

"I have a confession, Oliver," I admitted after a pregnant pause. "It's as much an acknowledgement to myself as it is an admission to you."

He smiled at me, his eyes roaming my face. "Tell me, darling."

"I could have lived anywhere in the world, yet I chose to stay in London. I could have rented, but I chose to buy. I saw a million different flats in a million different neighborhoods, but I chose mine because of the easy distance between *us*. I timed it. It's seven minutes." I took a deep breath. "At night when I lay down, I can only fall asleep if I'm imagining myself here, in that bed," I said, nodding toward my old room, "with you by my side as we did that day. I stayed in London for you. *Because* of you. I want *you*. Only you."

Oliver swallowed and his hands fell to his sides. I angled my face up closer to his, a silent invitation. Hesitant at first, he hovered his lips over mine, and the warmth from his breath brushed across my cheeks.

Slowly, tortuously, his lips met mine. An explosive rush of blood erupted through my veins, carrying with it emotions I had never felt, excitement I had never experienced, an intoxication so drugging I wondered if I was meant for death. And I would have welcomed it. I would have happily accepted it if it meant his lips on mine, even if it was for just the one time.

Oliver's hands went to my back and he pulled me into him, shifting his mouth over mine over and over with languid turns of his lips. His fingers found my hair and threaded there, pulling slightly, and sending shivers down my spine. He broke away and kissed down my jaw, tugging softly at my hair, pulling my head back to expose my throat. He moved his mouth over the skin there, spilling down until he met my collarbone.

He pulled away, leaving me gasping for more. I buried my face in his neck, fistfuls of his shirt in my hands.

"Keep going," I whispered.

I felt the vibration of his laugh against my face and smiled. "If I keep on, love," his deep voice murmured, "I won't stop, and hell if I'll be that guy again." He pulled me away and tucked his hands beneath my jaw before running them up into my hair. He kissed beneath my ear once. "We have to leave," he told me, kissing me again at the corner of my mouth. "Now, or I won't be responsible for the inevitable."

I nodded into his mouth and teased his lips with mine, walking backward toward the door but bringing him with me. We kissed back and forth until my back hit the door and continued when his hand found the knob and turned. A small gasp escaped me when he whipped me around and opened the door, pulling us through, and closing it behind us, our mouths still intertwined.

He lifted me and walked me to the passenger side of his car, setting me down and breaking our kiss. He pressed my back into the side of his car and leaned into me.

"You're very good at this, Mr. Finn," I told him.

"I beg your pardon, Miss Beckett, but what is this man without this woman? I am what I am because of you."

My breath left my lungs in a rush. "Say more things like that," I ordered, making him smile.

He pressed his body deeper against mine and ran his hands throughout my hair, picking up a strand with one and wrapping it around a finger. "Thank you for choosing me," he said, making me melt beneath his fingertips. "That simple act has gained you a follower for life, Penelope Beckett. I'll do it, gladly. To the moon and back, to the ends of the earth, around your finger without cease, if that is your wish.

"May I ask you a question?" he asked.

"Yes," I answered.

"Could you fall in love with me?"

"Yes," I told him without hesitation.

"Would you?"

"Yes."

"Will you inform me the hour, the minute, the second you do?"

"The very moment," I promised.

He smiled his crooked smile, the one I'd noticed belonged only to me. "Let's get you home, darling."

Chapter Twenty

Oli drove me home and walked me to my door. When I let myself into my flat, he followed me in only to see that it was safe and left me with a simple kiss at my temple.

I went to bed that night in a euphoria I hadn't known could inhabit the earth. It was as if I was invited to a very private, very exclusive club no one is aware of until you're a member. And it was exquisite.

The morning of the show I texted George that I would be at Alice & Emma, which was preceded by an immediate phone call.

"Morning," I greeted, after sliding the answer button.

"You bagged that delicious boy, didn't you?" she asked without preamble.

"I did nothing like that!" I insisted.

"He dumped the blonde and came running to your side and now he's taking you to Alice & Emma."

"George! You make it sound so scandalous!"

"It is, love, but I've never shied away from such things,

you know this. I wholeheartedly approve. He is scrummy, sweetheart!"

"Oh, hush," I told her, laughing into the phone.

"And you're going to marry that bloke, I just know it. Little children will be scampering beneath your feet before you know it. You are so getting married."

"George! That's not true!" I exclaimed, before imagining that exact scenario, my stomach plummeting to my feet and back up at the satisfying thought.

"Bollocks, love, you know it is."

"George." I sighed, ignoring her. "I'll see you at the show?"

"Yes, wear something outrageous and shocking."

"You're insane!" I laughed. "See you there."

"See you. And Penelope?"

"Yes?"

"Just remember you look rubbish in anything peach."

I snorted and laughed. "Bye, George."

"Bye, sweetheart."

I hung up the phone and hopped in the shower, singing at the top of my lungs as I washed my hair.

"Penelope!" I heard over the running water.

"Oh shit!" I screamed. Startled, I dropped my loofah. "Claire! I'm in here!"

I heard her enter the bathroom and sit on my sink. "You're awfully chipper," she commented.

I pulled back the curtain a little and stuck out my head.

"I met up with Oli last night."

She sat up from her drooped stance. "Shut your face."

"He and his girlfriend broke up."

"Shut your face."

"He kissed me last night."

She hopped off the counter. "Shut your face!"

We both started jumping up and down and screaming, though mine wasn't as graceful standing behind a bunched curtain.

"I know!" I exclaimed when we settled down.

I shut the curtain and began to rinse my hair.

"What happened between yesterday afternoon after we talked until now?" she asked me.

"Dude, Claire, I went to dinner with Jasper—" I began, but Claire cut me off.

"Oh, how is he doing?" she asked, the tone of her voice a little too curious.

I globbed a bunch of conditioner in my hair and said, "He's good. He's great, actually, *why* do you want to *know*?"

"No reason," Claire mumbled.

I tucked the curtain back again and stared at her. "A fan of Jasper, are we?" I asked.

She started laughing. "You're a nutter!" she told the floor. "Why would you even think that? I have no clue why you'd even ask that. I only met him the once, and it was fleeting even then. I'm not a fan at all. I don't think he's charming or anything. I mean, it's not as if I find him handsome in the least..." she trailed off.

I barked a laugh. "Claire Bear! I am totally hooking the both of you up at tonight's party."

Claire's head whipped up. "He's coming to your party?"

"Of course," I told her.

"Have to go!" she said, scurrying out of my bathroom. "Love you! See you tonight!" She stopped at the doorway and turned around. "Oh, and Penelope?"

"Yes?"

"Happy birthday, my love."

I smiled at her. "Thank you, Claire."

Claire left in a flourish and I rinsed the conditioner out of my hair. I ransacked my closet for something to wear to Alice & Emma and decided to do something different for my vlog that day and film myself live. I got dressed, choosing a saucy little number, not in peach, thanks to George's prodding, and set my phone on a stand I bought for just such an occasion and went live.

"Good morning, my loves!" I greeted everyone.

As I did my hair, I filled everyone in on the night before. I told my viewers everything that went on in my life. Well, pretty much everything. I kept the night I fled Oliver's a secret because it was too sore a subject and I didn't want to humiliate him, but other than that, they were privy to pretty much anything. I told them about the searing kiss at his house the night before and almost swooned right out of my chair. I went into great detail about what we were doing that day, our breakfast that morning, and let them know about my birthday party that night, promising another live update then. By the time I was done, my hair and makeup were completed and I signed off with a flourish and a promise that I'd fill them all in later.

With butterflies in my stomach, I grabbed my Zoe and I made my way downstairs, hailing a taxi just in time outside. I piled inside and told him to take me to the Regency. I was having breakfast with Oliver.

Now, I'd eaten there a thousand times with him when I'd been with Graham, but not once had I ever looked as forward to eating there as I was that morning. It was all Oliver.

When the cabbie pulled up to Regency, I threw cash over the seat, thanked him, told him to keep the change, and sprinted out the door toward the restaurant all bright eyed and bushy tailed.

"Excuse me," I told a waiting patron.

I meandered through the thick crowd on the sidewalk and searched the faces for Oliver's, finally spotting him at a far corner between the restaurant and the shop next door. He looked casual and unhurried, his hands in his pockets, his back pressed against the window. He was beautiful.

His face lit up when he saw me approach. He stood from his leaning position, straightening his jacket and tie, and smiled at me.

"Hello, Penny Lane."

"Hello, Oli Oli Oxen Free." I smiled back.

He reached out for me and my heart sped up. He took me by the elbow and kissed my cheek, lingering there for a moment and sending a thrill down my spine.

"I'm happy to see you, love."

My hand went for his chin and I brought his mouth to mine for a quick kiss in answer.

He stood, wrapped his arm around my waist, and presented our buzzer. "I've already put our names on the list half an hour ago."

"You've been here for half an hour? You should have told me, I would have come sooner."

"I didn't want you to have to stand in whatever ludicrous shoes you've burdened yourself with today, knowing we had loads of standing later." He cocked his head forward to take a gander at my feet. I lifted a shoe in the air. "Just as I suspected, utterly ridiculous."

"I bleed for fashion."

"Literally," he said, examining the tip of my shoe. "One swift kick with these and the receiver would be a goner," he joshed.

I playfully pushed him and laughed. "They're multipurpose."

Oliver's eyes traveled up my legs and hips, all the way up to my face. "You look enticing, Penelope."

"You're not too hard on the eyes either, Oliver Finn."

He tightened the knot of his tie. "I try."

"No, you don't," I teased him. "You shower and shave and dress and are done in half an hour tops."

He barked a laugh. "It's a bit more than that, love."

"You see this?" I started, gesturing down my body. His eyes cascaded down my figure once again and my whole body shivered. "This is an hour and a half. On a good day," I eked out.

"A *very* good day indeed," he flirted.

"Your Casanova is showing," I ribbed.

His eyes became very serious. "It's not a line, Pen."

I gulped nothing. "Oh," I breathed.

His right hand found my elbow and slid slowly down my arm then laced his fingers with mine.

"I have a confession," his proper accent informed me.

I turned toward him slightly, keeping our hands together. "Oh yeah, what's that?"

"I've been seeing a therapist."

I was shocked by this. "Have you? For how long?"

"Five months now. It took a while for me to break open to her. I was, of course, ashamed and embarrassed, then suddenly I wasn't." He paused, but I didn't interrupt. He continued, "I told her everything—starting with Brooke, how we met, how we fell in love, how I had no clue she had been cheating on me, and how she ultimately took her own life.

"I told her about my behavior after her death." He looked at me. "I told her about you."

I swallowed. "What did you say?"

"That I found someone I thought extraordinary."

"I'm extraordinary?"

"Without a doubt," he whispered.

I stared up at him, afraid to speak.

"Am I frightening you?"

"Not anymore," I told him without hesitation and meant it.

"Are you a patient woman?" he asked.

"As a saint." I smiled.

"I'm coming to terms with things I've let alone for too long now. I'm mourning the loss, so to speak. I'm learning to forgive myself for things that aren't necessarily my fault." He smiled that crooked, knowing smile. "Or so my therapist says."

"Like what?" I asked him, letting my thumb slide back and forth across the top of his hand.

"I blame myself for Brooke's death."

I let out a shaky breath. "That's heavy."

Oliver's brows furrowed. "We can talk of other things," he offered.

"You think this makes me uncomfortable?" I asked.

"Doesn't it?"

"No," I answered. "This is your life, and I want to be in it, Oli."

"And you're certain of that?"

"Very."

"Why?" he asked me. "Why would you want to be in my messy, complicated life, Penelope?"

"Too many reasons to mention, really, but mostly because you fit me so perfectly. You're interested in me, really interested. There is nothing more attractive to a girl than a boy who genuinely cares for them."

"I am and I do," he admitted.

"I know this. Now, go on," I prodded.

He nodded. "If I had been paying attention to her the way a husband should, I would have seen it coming. At least that's what I feel, anyway. My therapist doesn't agree."

"People are very good at keeping secrets, especially explosive ones."

"That's what my therapist says," he told me. "That people are only as revealing as they want to be." He looked at me. "But it kills me that she didn't want me to see her. I told Dr. Artiles, my therapist, that she might not have cheated if she could have only been open with me about what was causing her to drift toward the idea of it."

"What did your therapist say?"

"That she might have done it regardless and we can't predict false futures. We can't argue our way into different results."

"And?"

"And that it wasn't my fault."

I let go of Oliver's hand and placed my palm against his cheek. "It wasn't your fault."

He smiled sadly at me. "Then why do I feel so guilty?"

"Because you cannot fix something that is beyond

repair, Oliver, and I think that eats away at you like nothing else."

He breathed deeply. "I can finally admit this out loud," he said, his eyes meeting mine. "It had devastated me."

"Suicide is so horrid in so many ways. The soul can't repent. Its death takes away with it all that had ever been good and places a harsh brand on everything it had ever touched. It takes all that was beautiful and tints it blue. Memories can never be remembered as they truly were. Love was never fully satisfied and sits unfinished. Love *begs* to be fulfilled. It is a cruel foe not just for the victim but for those that loved them."

"Penelope, you've spoken all I've ever wanted to say."

"My cousin took his own life," I explained. "My family, especially his mother, were never quite the same again. It's as if a black tide nips at our heels, screaming out his name, but every time we saunter in to find him, the water retreats. There is nothing like that helplessness. It feels hopeless."

"I'm sorry," Oliver told me.

"I pray for him every day. Just as you do with Brooke."

"It's the only power I have left," he said.

"What else has your therapist told you?"

"That my licentious ways might be caused by PTSD."

"I can see that," I told him.

"Or I could just be a right bastard," he disparaged himself, trying to make it into a joke.

"Are you?" I asked him point-blank.

He smiled and opened his mouth to tease me into changing the subject, but I interrupted him.

"Tell me," I insisted. "Are you?"

His smile fell and he swallowed. "I don't want to be. It

terrifies me that that man is who I really am."

"Why?"

"Because then I could never deserve you."

"As if I'm devoid of fault?"

"You are."

"You think and speak foolishly," I told him. "No one is perfect, especially me."

The buzzer in his left hand alerted us that our table was ready. Oliver gripped my hand and led me through the lingering crowd to the front where the hostess took us to our little table in a corner beside a few windows looking out onto a busy London street. We sat and Oliver ordered coffee from a sweet waitress we'd both had hundreds of times. I ordered tea. We knew the menu already and gave her our order.

"Never seen the two of you in 'ere together," she commented. She eyed me with suspicion. "Aren't you with that fair-headed chap?"

"Not since he cheated on me with a French floozy," I quipped.

She burst out laughing. "Went for 'is friend then, uh? Good on you," she said, walking away.

"You're such a hussy," Oli provoked.

"Shut up, punk, or I'll make up some outrageous lie about you and tell her."

"You wouldn't."

"I would."

"Just for shits and giggles, cough up. What would you tell her then, hmm?"

I placed my elbows on the table and drummed my fingers together. "I'd say that we weren't dating. That we'd actually just come from burying his body and this was the celebratory breakfast before we both escaped to Mexico."

Oli cracked up. "You're impossible, Beckett."

"Impossibly awesome," I joked.

He smiled. "I wouldn't disagree."

I rolled my eyes.

"What?" He burst with a laugh.

"Save the cheese for the party tonight, son."

He shook his head playfully at me. His hand laid on the table between us. With unnecessary caution, as if he was still afraid of my rejecting him, he inched his hand toward mine. I didn't dare move my fingers with his. He needed to know he had to do all the work but I *wanted* him do it.

With Graham, I did all the apologizing, all the groveling, all the wanting, all the work. It got me none of the reaction I was begging for in him. Simply put, if a boy wants to love you, he will. You cannot force it. Trying to only makes you appear weak, and women are infinitely more powerful than they could possibly comprehend. It starts with a demand, a simple "you come to me." It's the most natural course of things and I thought I could alter it, but I failed.

With that failure, though, came a clarity I will forever be grateful to. With that failure, I learned to be most sure of myself, more comfortable with who I am, and what I expected from the opposite sex. I learned I was incredibly desirable *to the right boy*. I learned that his willingness to climb mountains for you should be clear in the manner in which he treats you, looks at you, and works for you. It's in the things he gives up for you, in the things he would slay dragons to get you. Love is inconvenient. Love is in the sacrifice.

Oliver's hand found mine, his fingers sought mine, his thumb caressed my knuckles. I rewarded him with a smile.

"I am not that man," Oliver promised me.

"I know this," I said.

"Then why ask?"

"Because I needed *you* to know it."

Oliver smiled at me.

"Well, isn't this charming?" a familiar sarcastic voice chimed over us.

My heart beat into my throat as I turned toward its owner.

"Graham, what can I do for you?" Oliver asked casually.

I tried to pull my hand away from Oliver's but he held tight.

"Nothing, really. Mates and I had a fast night and came here. Of course," he said, as their mutual friends Alfie and Charlie walked to stand next to Graham, "I wasn't expecting this tasty sight."

Alfie and Charlie nodded at me. I gave them each a small smile. They smirked at one another when they saw my hand in Oliver's. I tried yet again to pull away my hand but Oliver held strong.

"I'll call you later," Oliver said, making my stomach sink. I didn't want him to call him. Ever. Graham was a dirty boyfriend and a dirty friend. I wished Oli could see that.

Graham laughed and looked at me. "Dismissed so readily," he said. He smiled at me. It held all the false kindness I'd failed to notice during the eight months we'd seen one another. "You look smashing, Penelope," he oozed. "Surprised to still see you here in London, though."

"Thought I'd stick around for a while," I told him. "See what kind of trouble I could get into."

He laughed like it was funny for a very different reason other than my implied meaning and shook his head. "Trouble. Yes," he bit out.

I held back a quip about Chloe that had been sitting at the tip of my tongue. Instead, I refused to give in to his bait, and the look on his face when I didn't was satisfaction enough. He looked disappointed. In that silence, I let him know I never thought of him anymore. And I never would again.

"Goodbye, Graham," I said, turning back to Oliver.

Graham stood still, seething, staring at me, but I declined to acknowledge him. He stood for thirty seconds at least, waiting, but neither Oliver nor I gave in. Quietly, he turned from our table and joined Alfie and Charlie.

"Where were we?" Oliver asked.

***

When breakfast was over, we left for Alice & Emma and chose two seats in the back, two seats in the dark.

"Are you comfortable?" he asked me.

"Yes," I answered, placing my Zoe bag on the back of my chair.

"Pen?"

"Yes?"

"Last night, you said you were frightened of me."

"Yes."

"You frightened me as well. Still do," he admitted.

I shifted in my seat and faced him. My hand found the side of his face, his jaw scratchy from lack of razor. "You didn't shave this morning."

He swallowed and shook his head. "You're a forever girl."

"You never forget to shave," I said.

"What if I'm not of the forever kind?"

I looked at him, through and into him. "The forever kind don't inherit, Oli. The forever kind choose who they want to be, which one they want to be. You choose then develop the character to keep the choice."

"I want to be the forever kind, Pen. You make me want to be the forever kind. More than anyone I've ever met."

I thought this untrue. "You were the forever kind with Brooke, Oliver."

He shook his head. "I thought I was."

"You were."

He shook his head again, adamant. "I would have stayed forever, but I was never panicked I couldn't live up to the task like I am with you. There was never an urgency to please her like I have with you." He paused. "Does this make me a terrible person?"

My other hand found the other side of his face. "I don't think so, Oliver. You act like there is no humanity in the choices we make."

"I would have loved her forever, Pen, but I would have never burned for her as I do with you." This canon stole several heartbeats from me, ones I would never get back, ones I didn't care I'd lost. "That is the source of most of my guilt now. If I had let her find that with someone else, she might be alive today."

"*Oliver*," I whispered painfully.

"But I didn't know, Pen, I swear. I didn't know you could ache for someone the way I ache for you. If I'd known, I'd have let her go long before we married. Freed her to find her someone and then I would have sat quietly and waited for you happily. With the promise of Penelope Beckett, I would have waited forever."

Chapter
Twenty-One

Depression
    [dih-presh-uh n]
    noun
    1. sadness; gloom; dejection.

Penelope Beckett and Oliver Finn are about to get blindsided.

Oliver took me back to his house after the show. The party, which had excited me for so many days, felt like such a burden. Suddenly I wanted seclusion with Oliver. I wanted a world of two.

I helped him put up the silly luau decorations and arranged all the catered food he'd had brought in. It was all very generous. When all was up and laid out, we stood back and admired the results.

"This is very nice of you," I told him. "Thank you so much."

Oliver swung his hand into mine. "It's the very least I

could do," he said, bringing our folded hands up and kissing the tips of my fingers. "I hope it's okay but I've invited my family."

I gasped. "Of course it's okay! I'll be so happy to see them again, Oliver. I really loved your mom."

He smiled at me. "As she loved you, I suspect." He laughed. "I caught a lot of heat when we parted ways."

I giggled. "Aww, I'm sorry."

Oli looked at me seriously. "Don't be sorry. How it was is how it should have been, despite what I thought or said that day."

"So many times I wanted you to come to me. The months that followed, I had to prevent myself from calling," I admitted.

Oli stood still. "These last few weeks, I've thought of you constantly. If I'd known you were in London, Pen, I would have beat down your door."

"You'd have only needed to knock. I would have opened it for you."

"And yet," he countered, "this moment feels like kismet. I couldn't have guaranteed as much had it been a second sooner."

"Good things come to those who wait?"

"Very good things." He smiled.

The doorbell rang and Oliver went to answer, throwing a grass skirt my direction as he did. I giddily tied it around my waist and threw on a lei, grabbing the lot to help him greet partygoers. We said hello to friend after friend. George and the oh-my-gawd girls from FACE showed. Claire came, luckily, right as Jasper had, and I kissed them both on the cheek.

"Oh, Claire," I implored in front of him, "would you be

a doll and keep Jasper close? I'm afraid he doesn't know many here and I'll be playing hostess all night."

"I believe I can do that," she said, taking Jasper's arm when he offered it.

I winked at her as they passed, making her laugh.

"I'm hooking them up," I whispered to Oli.

He raised a sardonic brow at this but didn't say anything.

When his family arrived, I almost cried. I greeted each one with excitement, told them how pleased I was to see them, especially Sophia, Archie, and Imogen. His nieces and nephew had gotten so tall and mature since I'd seen them last and I told them so. Sophia squealed when I did.

"There has to be at least seventy-five people here!" I yelled over the booming music and chattering crowd. "I didn't even think I knew seventy-five people in London!"

"Apparently you do, love!" Oliver smiled then took my hand and spun me in a circle.

He swung me to him, our chests and stomachs pressed together. "I'm very happy," I declared.

This made him smile. "That's very good news."

"How so?"

"I can only be happy when you are, Pen."

"Are you happy then?" I asked.

"Deliriously so, darling."

I kissed his cheek then and dragged him onto the "dance floor," i.e. the connected dining to the kitchen, with the other dancers. Vampire Weekend's "Taxi Cab" rang through the room and I wrapped my hands around Oliver's neck. We swayed back and forth slowly, like time didn't count, as if the song would last forever.

"This is our first dance," he said.

I shook my head. "No, it's not."

He looked surprised. "I think I'd remember, Pen," he said. He turned pensive for a moment. "Oh that night in the Bray Village pub, but I don't count it."

"Neither do I, but I wasn't even referring to that one. Remember last year, we all went to that terrible pub in Kent to meet that random chick Alfie met in town the week before."

"Oh my God, yes, I remember that. Terrible night. We told him it wouldn't work, but he insisted."

Oliver searched the room for someone. "Alfie!" he yelled out. "Alfie!"

"Yeah, mate!" Alfie shouted back.

"Remember that useless night in Kent?"

"You promised, you wank!"

"She wanted none of you, yeah?"

"Shut it!" Alfie called back.

Oli turned back to me. "He's an idiot."

"I know," I agreed, laughing.

"So?" he asked.

"So, what?"

"The dance."

"Yeah. Anyway, it was late. We'd been there for hours and Alfie had gotten nowhere with that girl, just as we predicted, which made the trip even more worthless. I'd gotten bored and I begged Graham to dance with me, but he was in a foul mood and told me to piss off. Instead of ignoring me like the rest of them, you stood up, sloshed out of your mind, and you said—"

"I'll dance with you, Pen," Oli offered.

"That's right," I said softly.

"I barely remember. That's disappointing."

"We danced much like this," I explained.

"It was a slow song?" he asked.

I nodded. "It was two in the morning, our bodies lazy with fatigue and alcohol. You leaned into me and I remember thinking that if Graham had been paying any attention, he would have socked you in the face."

Oli smiled. "Alcohol removes all inhibitions."

"That night it *certainly* did. You flirted with stubborn persistence."

"I did, did I? Had any of it worked?" he teased.

I swallowed. "Yes," I acknowledged. "It had."

Oliver watched me for a moment. "No regrets?" he asked.

I smiled. "None."

Just then the doorbell rang with another guest. Oli sighed, kissed my cheek, promised to be right back, and went to greet the latecomer. I meandered a few feet toward the island with all the food, snagged an artichoke bruschetta, and took a bite. I took my appetizer and fell into one of the dining chairs Oli and I had pushed against the windows in the kitchen. I put my feet up onto the chair next to mine and ate peacefully, watching Oliver's parents with their grandchildren. Before long, Zoe sat near my feet.

"Hello, my love," she said. "Having a nice birthday so far?"

"You know, it's wonderful," I told her.

"I'm glad you're with our Oliver now," she told me. "If that wasn't obvious from the day we all met you," she added, giggling.

"I feel like it's all a bit of a dream," I admitted.

"Here's to that never ending," she said, raising her

champagne flute in the air and taking a sip.

Shouting came from the foyer and we both jumped up to see what the commotion was. It seemed the whole party had the same idea and we couldn't get through.

"What's happening?" I shouted to Alfie in the middle of the crowd.

"Seems Oli's gotten into a bit of a shouting match!" he told me.

"What?"

I pushed through the crowd, shedding my grass skirt and pulling off my lei, imploring them to let me across. Eventually I broke through to the end.

"Look, mate, you're drunk," Oliver told a staggering Graham. "Go home then and sleep it off. I'll ring you in the morning."

"What are you *doing* here?" I shouted at Graham, astonished.

"Pen," Oliver pleaded, "go back inside. I'll take care of this."

"How did you even know we were here?" I asked Graham, ignoring Oliver. I turned toward Alfie, who'd joined the crowd spilling out from the house and onto the sidewalk. "Did you tell him?" I found Charlie and the rest of the boys. "Did you?"

They all raised their hands and shook their heads no.

"*You* told me, babe," Graham hollered.

Oliver looked a bit betrayed when he heard this.

"I most certainly did not!" I yelled at Graham. "I did not," I told Oliver, my tone much quieter but firm.

Graham started laughing. "You did, though, love. In that ridiculous vlog of yours this morning, remember?"

I felt all the breath in my lungs leave at once. "You've

been watching my vlogs?"

"Of course," he said without further explanation.

"Please leave, Graham," Oliver asked. His face gave away how annoyed he really was, though. "We'll go back to our party and I'll talk to you tomorrow."

Oliver looked toward the street for a passing cab, but there were none.

"You're together now? The two of you?" he asked us.

Oliver looked at me then back at Graham. "Yes, we are," he told him.

"Isn't that amusing," Graham expressed.

He dug into his pocket and pulled out a pack of cigarettes. He brought one to his lips, which confused me. Graham had never smoked when we had been together.

"It was Chloe," he explained, reading my thoughts, and lighting up. He took a giant drag and turned his head toward the street, smoke billowing out from between his lips. "She insisted I start," he continued. "I always thought them vile things but she loved them. I figured if I couldn't get her to quit, I would start just so I didn't have to look past the smell of them." He barked out a short laugh. "Look where it's gotten me now, though, yeah? No more Chloe. Only, the habit's stuck."

I opened my mouth to tell him I was actually sorry to hear that he and Chloe had broken up. I surprised myself that I thought it and was even more amazed that I held no more resentment toward him now that I had Oliver. After all, I wouldn't have him without Graham's cheating ways. I was grateful as odd as that seemed.

"Graham," I began at the same time Oliver addressed him.

"Graham," Oliver parroted, "you have to leave, mate."

"Uh," Zoe told the party crowd, "let's all head inside. Let them work all this out," she said, ushering people indoors.

Soon it was just the three of us. Without the buffer of our guests, the tension was palpable. Graham watched me, swaying slightly, his eyes burrowed themselves into my skin, making me want to flee.

"You know he wanted you first?" he asked me, throwing a shoulder toward Oli. I refused to answer. "He wanted you first, which made me want you too. I called dibs, you know, and he gave in so easily. Like you were a piece of property." Graham started laughing then sighed. "That's what you are to us, Penelope. You're our property, our plaything."

"I belong to no one but me," I told him.

"Zoe!" Oliver yelled through the open door. "Can you ring up a cab, please?"

"Done!" she called back.

Graham took another drag from his cigarette. "Oh, you're our plaything. A proper plaything." He shook his head. "I didn't really even want you all that badly," he revealed, wounding me.

"Shut up," Oliver gritted out.

"I only took you because I knew you'd go for me, and this boy," he said, pointing to Oliver, the cigarette dangling between his fingers, "this *boy* you see in front of you, was such a fucking sap, he *let* me. What kind of man lets another man take like that?" Graham laughed again. "I'll tell you, Penelope Beckett. Your Oliver's that kind of man.

Oliver's jaw tightened, the sinewy tendons in his throat pulled taut, his eyes narrowed in careful control.

Graham ignored him. "That's why I'm here. I'm taking

you back, Penelope. I've developed a taste for you, it seems, and now I'm enchanted." He nodded like the egomaniac he was. "Yes, I think I'll take you back," he drunkenly slurred.

It was my turn to laugh. "You came here with nothing and you will leave with nothing."

"Come now, love, we both know you're only with him because you want to remain close to me. That's why you stayed in London. It's why you dug down with him. He's a poor man's Graham."

"Graham, that is enough!" Oliver shouted, his face a shock of red. "You're not welcome and you're done here!"

"Oooh, look at him go now," Graham sang, flicking his finished cigarette at his feet.

Oliver looked livid, his jaw set, his eyes narrowed. Without warning, he jumped forward and tossed Graham into the brick, his arm pressed into Graham's throat. "I've put up with a lot of *shit* with you, Graham! I've born some horrifying things from you, watched you do reprehensible things, but this is one that will not, *cannot* be tolerated. You had your chance with her, you *cheated* on her. How in the fuck could you do that to her? It's *Penelope*! She's gosh damn *Penelope*, Graham!"

Graham drunkenly pulled at Oliver's arm, but his arms failed to make purchase. He was having trouble breathing.

I walked toward them and looked into Oliver's eyes, tugging gently at his arm. "Let him go. Come back inside with me. Show me love in there. Far away from here."

Oliver watched me and nodded once, relaxing his arm. He let Graham fall to the ground. I grabbed him around the waist and we started to ascend the steps to the door.

"You threw yourself down that sunken terrace, Penelope," Graham quipped, out of breath, as we reached the door. "Oliver even thought so. We all had a good laugh about it at the pub the next week. Remember, Oliver?"

I looked up at Oliver, feeling hurt.

"I did not do that, Pen. None of us did. He's lying," Oliver assured me calmly.

"We all thought you were trying to off yourself," Graham prodded.

"I was not," I explained to Oliver. "It was an accident, pure and simple."

"I know," Oliver said softly.

His hand went to push open the door farther.

"When I found out what you'd done," Graham tormented, "I thought *I've done it again*."

Oliver and I froze where we stood. My breath sped in my chest. My hand held tightly to Oliver's arm.

Oliver slowly turned around, breaking my hold, but I couldn't find the courage to do the same. We stood facing one another, side by side.

"Whatever do you mean by that?" Oliver demanded of him.

I felt Graham climb a few stairs behind me. "I had no idea I had such a strong effect on women."

"What the fuck do you mean by that!" Oliver roared, descending two steps toward him.

"Put it together, Oliver," Graham baited.

"No," I whispered in disbelief. I turned to Graham. "No," I insisted.

"Oh, yes," he confirmed with a bristling smile, teetering on the edge of the stair he stood on. "I'd flirted with Brooke many times. Never thought she was into it, always calling me 'blockhead' and whatnot, but one day, I got her. One day Oliver was working late and she'd just joined the lads at the pub, pissed at him, and I knew I'd get her. She melted beneath my touch that first night."

"Shut your mouth," Oliver seethed.

"Then it was everything I could do to keep her off of me," he kept on but turned, for some reason addressing me. "We'd meet mostly during lunches, or the occasional night he worked late. Eventually the guilt weighed too heavily on her and she broke it off. It wasn't a month later she jumped onto those tracks."

"You goddamned asshole!" Oliver yelled, pushing him off the stairs.

Graham toppled backward, his back hit the sidewalk in a deafening thud, yet he laughed, pleased with his sick game.

I bolted through the door yelling for Alfie, Charlie, and the other boys. They whisked past me just as Oliver had reached Graham, his hands around his throat.

The rest of the house came spilling out and around us, people yelling, trying to figure out what was going on. I sat at the edge of the stairs, my hands on my knees.

"You killed her!" Oliver yelled at Graham. "You murdered her!"

"What's happened?" Zoe asked me before turning toward the front door again. "Mum, can you just take the kids to Oli's room then?"

Zoe looked at her brother shouting at the top of his lungs at Graham, both men held back by their friends who looked shell shocked, trying to figure out what was going on themselves.

I stood and faced Zoe. "Brooke's affair?" I swallowed. "It was with Graham."

Zoe's mouth dropped open. "Oh, God help us," she said, her hand going to her face.

Oli's dad, George, came down the stairs, looking confused. "What's this Eleanor's on about a fight?"

"Brooke's affair was with Graham," Zoe revealed.

George looked like she'd hit him in the head with a shovel. He was stunned and speechless.

I left them on the stairs and cut through the mass.

"What's happened, then? I can't make it out," Alfie shouted over them at me.

"Enough!" I yelled at the two of them. The night grew quiet. I lifted a hand toward Graham. "How could you do this, Graham?"

"This is life, love. Shit happens."

I shook my head in disgust at him. "This isn't *life*. This is horrifying."

Oliver threw his arms out to shake off his friends. His hands formed fists at his side. "How could you go out with me night after night? How could you call me your friend all the while you were having an affair with my *wife*?" he bellowed. Gasps sounded throughout the group. "How could you listen to me drone on and on about her death? How I thought it was all my fault? How could you let me stew in that guilt, Graham? You were supposed to be my friend."

"We are friends, mate," Graham said softly.

"No, I'm just discovering that we are very far from friends. No, we are enemies. The difference is that I didn't know that fact until now." He glanced at me. "I *lost* her because of you. *All that time*."

Seeing Oliver so distraught made me inexplicably sad for him. I wondered how he could ever look at me without seeing Graham's face. And with that, my stomach started to tie in painful knots.

"You will never be happy, Graham," Oliver promised. "Never. Would you like to know why?" he asked, but didn't wait for an answer. "Because happiness cannot spring from selfish, and that's all you'll ever be. Since you never think of anyone else, never think of the consequences of your actions, since you are obsessed with pleasing only yourself, and you get your jollies off destroying others, you will never be happy. You aren't merely selfish, Graham, you're evil. Only an evil person could do what you've done and feel no remorse. Only an evil person could stay friends with the man whose life he ruined. You are without a doubt the most terrible person I've ever known.

"You've cost me more than any man should have to pay. If I never see your face again, it will still be too soon." He turned to Alfie. "Get him out of here. Now."

Alfie yanked Graham by the collar toward the lot where he parked and disappeared around the corner. At that moment, the cab Zoe called for Graham showed. Oliver looked at the people amassed around him but his eyes never found mine, leaving me colder than I've ever felt.

"I have something I need to do," Oliver told the sidewalk before walking over to the cab and settling inside.

I warred between wanting to chase after him and letting him alone. By the time I decided, it was too late to go after him.

"I think it's time everyone went home," Zoe told the astonished crowd.

Claire found me and threw me in a hug. "Come home with me," she said.

I shook my head. "I have to go find him."

Claire nodded. Jasper came forward and hugged me quickly. "Dude, what the hell? Graham is screwed up."

I felt my eyes burn. "I know."

"Do you want us to help you?" he asked.

I shook my head. "No, go," I said, forcing a smile. "I'll find him soon enough. Go, take Claire out somewhere nice. Kiss her at her doorstep. Exchange emails. Go."

He smiled sweetly at me, kissed my cheek, and I watched them walk off together. I kissed all my guests goodbye at the door and helped Zoe clean up the house for Oli. We were giving him space, time, but when the clock approached midnight, I'd had enough waiting. I'd had enough hoping without action and I left Oliver's sleeping family and caught a cab to the tube station Brooke had jumped from.

"Gloucester Road Station, please," I ordered the cabbie.

Somehow I was certain he would be there.

I touched my Oyster card to the pad and descended the stairs. With my heart in my throat, I searched the edge platform but couldn't see him. I had been so sure he'd have been there. I leaned against the wall and removed my phone. It had died hours before, but I attempted to start it up again out of desperation. It refused, so I placed it back in my bag, threading my hands through my hair. I watched as a train rode by. *Click, click. Click, click. Click, click.* The engine revved as it gained speed and left the station, a whirring melody tumbling behind it.

And there was Oli on the other side of the platform, facing me across the tracks. I stood and walked toward the edge, stopping just short of the painted yellow line and its *mind the gap*.

"Where you're standing," he said, "that's where she jumped."

I took two involuntary steps back as if the fate of that day still lingered in that spot.

"I'm so sorry, Oliver."

He shrugged his shoulders. "How could she have fallen for Graham's tricks?" he asked no one.

"He's very convincing," I answered anyway.

Oliver looked startled. "I forget you fell for his deceptions just as she had."

Two tears escaped and spilled over my cheeks. "We did."

"I'm sorry for you both."

I shook my head at him. "You don't have to feel sorry for me, Oli."

"Oh, but I do," he said. "You were caught up in our disaster and we whirled you about us without bracing you for the damage. I can't believe I was party to that, to a second victim."

"You're only a victim if you allow yourself to be."

He stared at me. "You are stronger than her, it seems."

"Not necessarily. I didn't know her. I only know she must have felt as if she had no alternative. I don't know the demons she struggled with. Only God knows that. All I know is that because of Him a-and because of you, there is nothing I wouldn't want to live for."

A train broke through our conversation, coming to a stop on his side. People unloaded and loaded, strolling in and around our suspended conversation. I could feel the words breaking up, twirling about our heads. I braced myself for their landing as the train pulled away, steeling myself for what I knew was going to be something extraordinary and difficult.

"I'm sorry for the hole Graham has created."

Oliver studied me. "Do you feel responsible to answer for him?"

I didn't know what to say, how to respond. In a way, I did. In a way, I didn't. Instead of answering, I asked, "When you look at me now, do you see him?"

"No," he answered.

This made five additional tears drip down my cheeks. I counted each one. "I can't tell you what it means to hear you say that."

He looked at me with softness. "How could I?" he asked. "When you are the sun and the moon and the stars. When you are everything bright and lovely, Penelope. You are his antithesis, but more importantly, you are your own soul, completely removed, severed from his poison and no longer subject to his stain. You are washed clean by none other than your own nature. You surpass him. You always have.

"Your lips and teeth speak only love," he continued. "No, I could never see him and you in the same place. I never have. I see you alone, Penelope. I see no other. You are all I see."

I gasped a watery breath and sobbed.

"Oliver."

"Yes, dearest?"

"This is the hour, the minute, the *second*."

He offered a smile. "This is the moment?" he asked.

"This is it."

Another train came bounding through on my side, rolling to a stop, as my heart pounded against my ribs. I felt desperate as passengers descended around me, taking with them the seconds that had belonged to Oliver. All my seconds belonged to him, would belong to him. I knew this with certainty.

The train fled the station but there was no Oliver on his side of the tracks. I peered up the center stairs but couldn't see him.

All at once, I was turned into a winded chest, a storm of emotions pouring all about us, peeling in layers of joy, sorrow, grief, desire, despair, pride, respect, and happiness, but most of all a passionate love.

"I love you, Penelope Beckett," Oliver Finn promised, and he kissed me as if the world was ending.

Acceptance
    [ak-sep-tuh ns]
    noun
    1. the act of taking or receiving something offered.

Penelope Beckett accepts Oliver Finn's offer.

Six months later...

"Scoot over, babe," I told Oli.

Oli laughed then glanced to his right. "There is literally not an extra inch I could move, love."

"Well, it's either find the room or we move because my derrière can't wedge into this infinitesimal space."

"You'll have to settle for my lap then," he said, leaning back, and bringing back a memory from long ago.

I tsked. *"God,* help me."

Oli mock gasped. "You've blasphemed in a house of the Lord. Ten lashings on the rear when we get back to my house, I'm afraid."

I shook my head. "You wish."

Oli leaned into me. "I most certainly do," he whispered.

"Control yourself," I ordered with a smirk.

"Or, perhaps, you could *make* me."

I stifled a laugh. "Oli, what's wrong with you?"

He smiled at me. "I can't help it. You can't look so fetching without a reaction from me. It's not right."

"Duly noted. From now on, it's burlap and burlap only from here on out."

He shook his head. "You can't, love. Your followers would never stand for it."

I raised a brow at him. "You've got this all figured out, haven't you?"

"Yes," he said.

The soft piano music that had been playing came to an end, indicating we needed to stand. The congregation rose with a flourish, their pews creaking with the effort, and turned toward the ancient church doors. They swept open as a pair of violins began to sing the "Swedish Wedding March," with its melancholy, beautiful, yet hopeful tone. It defined Jasper and Claire so well. With immediate tears, I took a staggering breath as Claire descended the aisle in a white silk gown with a dragging train, which seemed to roll along the stone beneath her feet, gathering all the good that had ever fallen there. Below her flowered crown, a smile befitting the happiest bride I had ever seen rested on her lovely face.

Oliver looked at me, but I was too satisfied in the match to care I was crying. His brows bit together in concern, his finger finding an unwieldy tear, catching and wiping it away.

"I always cry at weddings," I whispered.

"That may be true," he whispered back, "but that is not your cause today." He smiled. "These are the tears of a dear friend."

I smiled up at him. He took my hand and squeezed it.

Oliver looked at Claire. "You can't even tell she's expecting."

I stifled a gasp. "*What!*" I whisper-yelled. "How did you know?"

Oliver gave me a sarcastic smile. "They've only been dating for a few months, half that time he's back in LA, then suddenly he makes a massive move here and they get married in less than a month?" he whispered in my ear.

I bit my bottom lip. "I suppose it feels a little obvious, but they do love one another."

"I have no doubt of that," he stated.

"They want to do things correctly now."

Oli smiled. "That's sweet, Pen." I nodded. "Until the kid does the math."

I snorted to hold back my laughter.

"Shh!" a woman behind me scolded.

My face flamed and my mouth dropped open. "You got me in trouble."

"I have no idea what you're talking about," he teased.

Oli leaned into me and placed my hand in his as Claire and Jasper exchanged vows. "It's rather pretty, that promise."

"Mmm, yes. They exude something so sweet, so tangible, I feel like I could reach out into the air and bottle it up," I said.

We watched as they exchanged rings, their first kiss as husband and wife, and when the minister introduced them to the world as married, we all stood and cheered. Jasper and Claire walked back down the aisle as one.

When Claire reached us, she placed her hand on my cheek and smiled.

I placed my hand on hers. In a choked voice, I told her, "Congratulations, Mrs. Turner."

Once the wedding party exited behind the happy couple, people started moving in droves to leave the church.

Oliver grabbed my hand and held me there. "Stay," he said, "sit. Let the crowd clear. We'll catch up soon enough."

I moved beside him once more and we sat in that unhurried manner, the morning sun seeping through the tall stained glass windows, piercing the pews and people milling around us. I watched Oliver beside me. A single ray found his eyes, making them transparent. I peered closer as if I could see through them all the way into the depths of his soul.

"What are you looking for?" he asked me.

"I can see forever, you know. It's right there in your eyes," I told him.

"Can you now?" he whispered.

"That I can."

"What if I told you that all you saw, you could have?" he asked.

"Forever is a generous gift, Oliver."

"No, no. It's much more selfish than that, Penelope."

I smiled at him, but his face stayed deliberate and my smile fell.

My breath caught in my throat. "Why don't I think you're teasing now, Oliver?"

He sat up and leaned over me, his face inches from mine. "I am perfectly serious, Miss Beckett," his deep voice crooned. "Would you have forever with me? Would you sit beside me just as you are now, in this manner, in this church, in this pew, for all the days of our lives?"

My smile found my face once more. "Happily, sir."

"Then so be it, my darling," he replied, cementing eternity. Oliver kissed me sweetly then, clenching his hand in mine. He gestured to the cross hanging at the front of the church. "What a gift He gave me in you, though I am wholly underserving."

"None of us are," I told him.

He smiled and kissed my temple. "What an adventure we will have," he promised, then looked at me. "What an unbelievable adventure it's been." We sat silent for at least a minute. "Have you absorbed it then?"

With glassy eyes, I replied, "I think so."

"We're getting married, Pen," he stated softly, clutching me to him.

"I will be your bride, Oliver."

"And I, your groom." He shifted in his seat and reached into his jacket pocket. "I have a ring for you. Your mum helped me pick it out, and I've been walking around with it for weeks now." He pulled out a wooden box and pried open the lid. I reached for the ring, but he beat me to it. "Let me," he said, pulling it from its pillow.

Oliver Finn slid the ring onto my shaking finger. "There now," he said, "where it belongs."

"It's breathtaking, Oliver," I whispered.

"It's befitting then." I smiled up at him. "What say you

to a Christmas wedding, Pen?"

"I say that would be lovely."

"Pen?"

"Yes, Oliver?"

"I have chosen to be the forever kind."

"A very good choice, Oliver."

"And Pen?"

"Hmm?"

"I love you."

Epilogue

..."How are the kids, yeah?" Claire asked.

"Great, Claire, they're great. Growing like weeds."

"That's brilliant, Penny. Give my love to Oliver."

"And my love to Jasper."

Would you like to read more Fisher Amelie?
Visit fisheramelie.com

Visit FisherAmelie.com

Please, call the National Suicide Prevention Hotline:

1-800-273-TALK

* * *

Or chat with someone online: http://
www.suicidepreventionlifeline.org/

Life is worth living, you are not alone, and the way you feel is nothing to be ashamed of. *Trust me.* - Peace and love, Fisher Amelie

Listen to Fisher Amelie's Spotify and search Penny in London.

My card, darling...

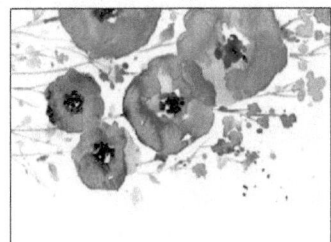

PENELOPE BECKETT
PennyinLondon.com

#55 Cherry Street
London
WC1E 7HU

Beckett.Comma.Penelope@gmail.com